W9-CDU-829

ACTS OF GOD

Also by ELLEN GILCHRIST

Acts of God

STORIES

Ellen Gilchrist

ALGONQUIN BOOKS OF CHAPEL HILL 2014

Published by
ALGONQUIN BOOKS OF CHAPEL HILL
Post Office Box 2225
Chapel Hill, North Carolina 27515-2225

a division of
WORKMAN PUBLISHING
225 Varick Street
New York, New York 10014

"Miracle in Adkins, Arkansas" first appeared (under the title "After the Storm")
in *Good Housekeeping,* © 2012 by Ellen Gilchrist. "Toccata and Fugue in D Minor"
first appeared in *China Grove,* © 2013 by Ellen Gilchrist. "Jumping Off Bridges into
Clean Water" first appeared (under the title "The Bridge") in *The Washington Post
Magazine,* © 2009 by Ellen Gilchrist. "Hopedale, A History in Four Acts"
first appeared in the *Arkansas Literary Forum,* © 2005 by Ellen Gilchrist.

This is a work of fiction. While, as in all fiction, the literary perceptions
and insights are based on experience, all names, characters, places, and incidents
either are products of the author's imagination or are used fictitiously.

LIBRARY OF CONGRESS CATALOGING-IN-PUBLICATION DATA
Gilchrist, Ellen, [date]
  [Short stories. Selections]
  Acts of God : stories / by Ellen Gilchrist.—First edition.
    pages cm
  ISBN 978-1-61620-110-4 (alk. paper)
  I. Title.
  PS3557.I34258A65 2014
  813'.54—dc23   2013043330

10 9 8 7 6 5 4 3 2 1
First Edition

To Susan Ramer, Standard Bearer, Friend

We were born of risen apes, not fallen angels, and the apes were armed killers besides. And so what shall we wonder at? Our murders and massacres and missiles, and our irreconcilable regiments? Or our treaties whatever they may be worth; our symphonies however seldom they may be played; our peaceful acres, however frequently they may be converted to battlefields; our dreams however rarely they may be accomplished. The miracle of man is not how far he has sunk but how magnificently he has risen. We are known among the stars by our poems, not our corpses.

—ROBERT ARDREY

CONTENTS

Acts of God

Because of the hurricane on the coast, the sitter was two hours late to the McCamey house that Saturday morning. The hurricane had not affected Madison, Georgia, but it had affected the sitter's son who had made the mistake of moving to New Orleans the year before. So the sitter had been on the phone all Saturday morning trying to placate her sister in Texas who had taken the son and his girlfriend in and was getting tired of them, especially the cats which the girlfriend had insisted on bringing to the sister's house.

Because the sitter was late, Mr. William Angus McCamey

and Mrs. Amelie Louise Tucker McCamey were alone from seven on Friday night until ten forty-five on Saturday morning, after which it didn't matter anymore whether the sitter was watching out for them.

"I can't stand the bacon she buys," Amelie had begun by saying, at six that Saturday morning when she was trying to get some breakfast going on the new stove her daughter, Anne, had moved into their kitchen the week before. "It won't crisp no matter how long you cook it."

"It's the milk that gets me," Will joined in. "I'd just as soon go on and die as drink that watered-down milk she gets."

"Cream," Amelie added. "It doesn't hurt to have cream for the coffee."

"Let's make some real coffee," Will said. "I'll make it. Where's our percolator." He opened a cabinet and got out the old percolator they had bought together at Lewis Hardware forty years before and took it down and went to the sink and rinsed it out and filled it with water and found the real coffee behind the sugar and started measuring it in.

Amelie passed behind him on her way to get some paper towels for the bacon and he stopped her and put his hands on her back end and held them there. "Bad boy," she said. "Let me finish with this bacon."

AMELIE AND WILL had been in love since the eighth grade at Madison Junior High when Will was the quarterback of the junior high team and Amelie was a cheerleader in a wool skirt that came down below her knees and a white wool sweater with a large M just in front of her new breasts. This was back when cheerleaders watched the football games and only got up to cheer when the team was having a timeout.

THE MADISON JUNIOR High was a three-story brick building on Lee Street, and it was still in use as a grade school, kindergarten through sixth grade. Many of their fourteen grandchildren and twelve great-grandchildren had gone to school there. Their great-grandchildren played in the school yard where Will gave Amelie her first kiss and where he had pushed her on the swings when the swings were twice as high as the safe ones they have now.

It was in a neighborhood that still boasted mansions and pretty wooden houses, but the houses were inhabited now by people who commuted to Atlanta and weren't from old Madison families like the McCameys and the Tuckers and the Walkers and the Garths. None of the new people belonged to the Daughters of the American Revolution, much less the Children of the Confederacy, and none of them ever came by to say hello to Will and Amelie or tell them they lived in the neighborhood.

Will and Amelie still lived in the white wooden house their daddies had bought for them the week it was discovered they had run off to South Carolina to be married, and with good cause, after what they had been doing after football games the fall they were seniors in high school. Will was the quarterback of the high school team and Amelie had given up being cheerleader to be the drum major of the marching band. Amelie and Will had been in love so long they couldn't remember when it began, although Will said he remembered the first kiss and how the leaves were turning red on the maple trees on the school yard. "They couldn't have been turning red," Amelie always said. "I had on a blue cotton dress with yellow flowers embroidered on the collar. I would not have been wearing that to school in October."

AT EIGHTY-SIX THEY were still in love and they did not forget what they had done on the front seat of Will's daddy's Ford car or on the screened-in porch of Amelie's Aunt Lucy's house in the country.

Walkerrest, the house was called, with two r's, and it was there that things first got out of hand. Amelie was caring for her aunt one football weekend while her aunt's husband was at a Coca-Cola board meeting in Atlanta. The aunt was crippled from a childhood illness and had no children of her own, but she had a face as lovely as an angel's and never complained or blamed God for having to stay in a wheelchair most of the time.

Will and Amelie did not forget that night at Walkerrest, or later, lying in bed in their new house with Amelie's stomach the size of a watermelon, sleeping in the four-poster bed in the house where they would live for seventy years.

The first baby was a boy named William Tucker so he wouldn't be a junior, and after him were Daniel and Morgan and Peter and Walker and then Jeanne and Jessica and Olivia and Anne.

In all the years Will and Amelie lived in the house they never went to bed without burying their hatchets and remembering they loved each other. They had a gift for being married and they were lucky and they knew it. They even kept on knowing it when their twin boys died at birth and had to be buried out at Walkerrest with their ancestors.

The sitter had come to live with them when they were eighty-four, a year after they had to quit driving and a year before they made their children get the sitter a house of her own.

"Or we shall surely go insane," Amelie protested. "She watches television all day long or listens to the radio. She is not always nice to us. We can not live with that all day and night."

"Night and day," William added. "We have telephones in every room. We won't both break our hips at once with no one looking. Or if we did then the laws of chance will have triumphed over human caution and we will accept our fate."

"Amen," Amelie said. "We can not have her here all day and night. We do not deserve this unkindness."

"We'll get a different lady," their daughter Olivia protested.

"They are all the same," Will said. "We have tried four. Each one is like the rest. Who would have such a job, watching old people to keep them from driving their car?"

"Or drinking sherry in the afternoon," Amelie added. "As if I ever had more than two small sherries at once in my life."

"All right," their daughter Anne agreed. "We will get her a place nearby and she can be here in the daytime."

"From ten until four," William bargained.

"From seven to dark," Anne said.

"A costly cruelty," Amelie charged.

"The insurance pays," Olivia said. "You know that, Momma. And you know we love you."

THE NEW SITTER program had been in place for seven months when Hurricane Katrina came across Florida and grew into a typhoon and slammed into the Gulf Coast of Mississippi and Louisiana and caused the sitter's son to flee to Texas with his girlfriend, causing the sitter to have to stay on the phone for two hours begging her sister not to kick them out until they found another place to stay. Then to sit and cry for another hour and dread going to the McCameys' house to have Mr. and Mrs. McCamey keep asking her to turn down the television set. I'll just stay home and watch the stories in my own house, the sitter told herself. I'm depressed from this hurricane and I hate my selfish sister and I wish her husband would just shoot the cats or take them to the woods and turn them loose. The sitter cried long and bitter tears and then opened a package of sweet rolls and sat down to watch the news on her own television set.

AT SEVEN THIRTY she called the McCameys' house to tell Mr. McCamey she would not be in until later in the day, perhaps not until afternoon.

At seven forty-five Will finished his third cup of coffee and polished off his eggs and told Amelie, "Let's go to the store. I am tired of that white-trash woman telling us what to eat. Let's go shopping."

"In the car?" Amelie asked, giggling.

"In our car," he answered.

THIRTY MINUTES LATER they were dressed and out in the garage climbing into the last Pontiac they had ever bought from Walker Pontiac on Elm and Main in downtown Madison. It was twelve years old and their son Walker had been begging them to give it to his grandson, but they had refused, writing a check for five thousand dollars to the boy instead. The McCameys' yardman kept it polished and ran the motor once a week and checked the oil and tires. It was dark blue and so comfortable that sometimes at night they backed it out of the garage and sat in it in the yard and cuddled up and talked about their children and the church and the state.

Now, on this sun-drenched Saturday morning with Amelie by his side, Will backed the Pontiac out of the garage, turned expertly around in the yard and drove out onto the street leading to the grocery store. The old grocery store was gone from that part of town, of course, and the new one was on a new road going south from town toward the new subdivisions being built by Little Buddy Scott, whose daddy had played ball with their son, Peter.

It was twenty minutes to the grocery store and they sailed along at twenty-five miles an hour and turned into the parking lot. Will got out and came around the hood and opened the door and helped his bride out of her carriage and she took his arm and they walked into the new Winn-Dixie store.

They had hardly made it to the produce section when they met a woman they knew who played tennis with their tennis-playing granddaughter. "Mr. Will," she exclaimed. "Miss Amelie. How good to see you. What are you doing at the grocery store?"

"Trying to buy some bacon and some ice cream," Will answered.

"We ran away from the wretched sitter," Amelie said. "Don't tell Anne on us."

"I never would," the woman said. "Let me walk around with you. I'll help you find things."

By the time the McCameys had their cart loaded with groceries they had a retinue of four young friends, all praising their courage and promising silence.

At the checkout stand there were seven people waiting to help them into the car. Jeannie Mayes and Margo Hight put the groceries in the backseat although Amelie would have preferred to have them in the trunk.

Their retinue stood gaily waving as Will and Amelie drove carefully across the parking lot and turned onto the road to home.

"Let's ride down and look at the new subdivision," Will said. "Just take fifteen minutes, there and back."

"Let's do," Amelie agreed and slid over beside him and put her hand on his thigh as she had always done all their years of riding in cars together. She slid it down toward his knee, of course, as she was a lady and to the manor born.

"LOOK AT THAT," Will said, as they approached the subdivision. "They're building a swimming pool at the foot of the hill. I'd never build a pool down there. Little Buddy must be going into debt on all of this. I heard he was in debt to every bank in Atlanta."

Will turned the wheel to drive in closer to the construction site. The fence had been taken down to make room for the tractors making the excavation and Will was able to drive right up to the beginning of the downcline. The sun was halfway up its arc in a clear blue Georgia sky. The sunlight on the windshield was brilliant and Will let it warm his face as it clouded his vision. His loins stirred at the warmth of Amelie's hand on his thigh, his heart turned over at the beauty of the morning. He touched the accelerator with a light foot as the front wheels went past the nonexistent berm and the Pontiac went straight down the incline and plowed into a concrete pillar. Amelie's hand pulled at the cloth of his pants and her head moved fast into the windshield and she was gone so fast she could not have counted to three. Mr. Will couldn't see the blood because he was not wearing a seat belt either and he had broken his neck on the steering wheel.

It did not hurt. It doesn't hurt, Mr. Will thought. Why doesn't it hurt? I think we are in the swimming pool, but there is no water and nothing hurts and that is that, I suppose, for now.

"Mr. Will," Little Buddy Scott was screaming. He had been climbing up onto a tractor when he saw the Pontiac fall into the pool. He climbed down from the tractor and came running like the flying halfback he had been, but it was too late. "Mr. Will," he screamed. "Can you open the door?"

Will raised his head a fraction of an inch from the steering wheel and looked into Little Buddy's blue-green eyes, just like his grandmother's had been. "There's ice cream in the back seat, Little Buddy. Be sure someone puts that in the freezer." Then he put his head back on the wheel and time stopped for him.

"A GOOD THING about trauma," the doctor told his sons and daughters. "It narrows the focus. It's the accident victim's friend. I doubt if he even knew it happened."

"It was the sitter's fault," Anne kept insisting. "I knew we couldn't trust that woman."

"You are too quick to blame," Walker told her. "The fault lies with the hurricane. She was tending to her family."

"They are gone," Olivia wept.

"The old fools," Jessica wept beside her. "They never listened to a thing but themselves in their whole lives."

"Don't say that out loud," her husband, David, cautioned. He was an Episcopal minister now, although he had been raised a south Georgia Baptist. He always tried to grab the high moral ground any chance he got. "Acts of God are not caused by human beings. They are of the Lord and he knows why he made them."

"Just leave me alone," Jessica said. "I'll say anything I like in my own mother's house."

"We're in the funeral home, Momma," her daughter put in. "We aren't in Grandmomma's house."

"How could they have done this to us," Jessica kept wailing. "After everything we did to make them safe."

"He told me to put the ice cream in the freezer." Little Buddy Scott drew near and joined the conversation. Jessica McCamey had been his Sunday School teacher and his ideal woman from the time he was seven until he was grown. He put his hand on her arm and looked deep into her eyes. "He was not in pain, Jessica, and your Momma was already dead. There are a lot worse ways to go when you are as old as they were. This could have been a blessing in disguise."

Jessica moved in nearer to him. She had always thought Little Buddy was a good-looking man. From the time he was a football hero until he started being a wealthy man she had

had her eye on him. Well, I'm sixty years old, she remembered. He's Jessica Anne's age, not mine.

"Thank you for coming to help them," she told him, letting him keep hold of her arm. "I have to accept this, I know, but it's taking time, Little Buddy. I was at the beauty parlor getting a manicure when they called me. Can you imagine what that was like?"

"I was climbing onto a tractor," he agreed. "And it was my swimming pool, my wall of concrete that was hardly dry."

"I was in my office," Walker said. "Anything can happen at any time."

"Let's pray," David offered. "Let's hold hands and say a prayer of thanksgiving for their lives. We're a family. Let's remember that we are one."

"Invite the sitter to the funeral," Jessica put in, to show off for Little Buddy what a nice lady she was. "Let's not forget her pain and guilty conscience."

While they were arguing and mourning and chattering and all the things human beings do with their wonderful voices and memories, especially in times of death, which is the worst thing they have to dread and contend and struggle with, the doors of the funeral home opened and the oldest son came in with his retinue. William Tucker had grown up to become a graduate of West Point and a four-star general and lived in Washington, D.C., and only came home for weddings and funerals. He came in wearing his uniform with his wife of forty years by his side and two of his sons and one of his daughters and her daughters. They were immediately surrounded by his brothers and sisters and taken into the adjoining room to view the bodies of his parents.

"A sad but brilliant death," he pronounced. "I didn't want Daddy to be an old man but this was more than I expected. What can I do to help?" he asked.

"Help us decide about pallbearers," his brother Daniel said. "There are so many children and they will all want to be one."

AT THE SITTER'S house the sitter was crying her heart out to her next-door neighbor. "It's all my fault," she wailed. "I was derelict. I didn't do my duty."

"They were old fools," the neighbor said. "Their children should have taken away the car. No one can blame you. You called them. You said you would be late."

"Late," the sitter wailed. "Oh, I was far too late."

"Well, they called and asked you to attend the funeral," the sitter's other neighbor put in. "I think you better start finding something to wear. I have a black dress if you don't have one."

"I can't go," the sitter said. "How can I show my face."

"They were old fools," the next-door neighbor said again. "Everyone knows that's true."

"I guess I will go." The sitter stood up. She brushed off her lap and pulled her shoulders back. She had just remembered a new brown cotton suit she had bought on sale at Penney's a week before. It might be sort of hot but it would look real nice at a funeral. She had to show her face. She couldn't look like she felt guilty and, besides, the McCameys had been nice. Except for making her turn down the television stories they had not done one single thing to make her hate them, which was more than she could say for most of the old people she had to watch.

"Good girl," her neighbor agreed. "Go wash your face and I'll make you a cup of coffee."

THE FUNERAL WAS very sad but very beautiful. Eight grandsons carried Amelie's coffin and five sons and a cousin carried William's coffin and they used the old service out of the old prayerbook and Lily Hight sang "Ave Maria" and the church was full and the day was bright and they carried the coffins out to the old cemetery on Walkerrest and laid the old people in the ground, and, except for Olivia, who kept taking tranquilizers for three weeks, grabbing her chance, they all went back to their regular lives. "To be alive becomes the fundamental luck each ordinary, compromising day manages to bury" was a saying Will had written on a piece of paper and stuck up on his dresser. After the funeral his youngest son, Walker, took it down and took it home and decided to remember what it said. He put the handwritten piece of paper up on his dresser in his bedroom and then he decided to make a list of all the people he was related to who were still alive as of September 11, 2005.

The list expanded and expanded and finally his wife, who had studied art at the University of Virginia, took all the names and dates he had collected and made them into a family tree. It was as large as a poster when they were finished with it and they had copies made and sent them as Christmas cards to many of the people whose names were part of the tree, of the branches and smaller branches, and everyone who saw it hanging on people's walls were reminded of life and its burgeoning and fruitfulness and joy and forgot for a while about death and sickness and old age.

After the youngest son and his wife made the large, beautiful, poster-size tree, they began to look around them at other families, at groups of people they didn't know, at large Mexican families at grocery stores and in malls, with a deeper understanding of what is going on in the world and how priceless and marvelous life is and to be cherished and protected in all its forms.

There is much we know that we forget, Walker kept reminding himself, so much goodness we must strive to remember.

Miracle in Adkins, Arkansas

The tornado struck in the middle of the night. It swept across an eight-block stretch of the small town of Adkins, Arkansas, and leveled dozens of houses.

At ten the next morning four teenagers from the Fayetteville, Arkansas, First Methodist Church Youth Group left Fayetteville headed south and east to Adkins to see if they could help. Their names were Jason Hall, Marie James, Hardin James, and Tommie Anne Farley. At the last minute they were joined by John Tucker Farley, whose Jeep Cherokee was the automobile they were driving.

They stopped at the big Walmart near the mall and picked up as much bottled water, warm clothes, and food as they could pack into the vehicle, then they started driving. They were dressed in long pants and were wearing hats and carrying work gloves. John Tucker and Jason had on hunting boots. The rest were wearing tennis and basketball shoes.

JOHN TUCKER AND Tommie Anne Farley's father was a weatherman on Channel Five and he had called several times to tell them it might be raining in Adkins on and off all day. "Spitting rain," he predicted. "So be prepared and take extra clothes. I went on one of these operations after a tornado in Oklahoma. The worst part is getting wet and cold. Let me talk to your mother."

"We have to go, Dad," John Tucker said. "Call us on the way if you find out anything new. Call Mom on the land phone. We need to leave."

John Tucker and Tommie Anne had excessively attentive parents. Both John Tucker and Tommie Anne had spent a lot of time developing skills for getting their parents out of their rooms or off of telephones. Later, in 2010, when John Tucker was involved in running a senatorial campaign for a physician in Springdale, he would be invaluable for his ability to get people off the telephone at campaign headquarters.

But I am getting ahead of this story, which is about a miracle that occurred on the ninth of April, 2008, in the small town of Adkins, Arkansas.

It was raining when they left Fayetteville, making it difficult to load the supplies into the Jeep at Walmart, but the Walmart checkers double-bagged everything and the greeters helped with the packing. They let John Tucker back the Jeep up to the front door where a twenty-two-year-old greeter named Zach Wells was just starting his shift. "I wish I could go with you guys," he told them. "I heard about the tornado on the radio driving to work. There are fourteen dead people already. It took out two churches, a school, and most of the downtown. It's the worst tornado in fifty years. The president of the United States is coming tomorrow. The governor is on his way."

"Well, we'll be there, too," Marie James said. She was handing double-wrapped packages to Zach and admiring the way he picked up the heaviest ones and fit them into the back of the Jeep.

"I hope it stops raining down there for you," Zach said. "It said on the radio it's still raining on the rescue effort."

"We know," Marie said. "Our driver's dad is the weatherman on Channel Five."

"Get in," John Tucker said. "Let's get going. It's going to

be crowded with all this stuff. Sit wherever you can find a seat belt."

In Adkins the Red Cross had trailers in place to register people coming to help. The Fayetteville Five, as they had decided to call themselves, were assigned to a squad that was searching wrecked neighborhoods for survivors or lost pets.

They spent the day pulling apart wrecked houses and moving debris. Everything they touched was soaking wet. All the boards had black nails showing through the wet wood. The predicted spitting rain came and went but none of them noticed it. There was too much destruction for rain to seem an issue. Bodies were being taken out on stretchers, lost dogs and cats were wandering around and being captured by an animal rescue team from Hope, Arkansas, and another from Morrilton. Houses had been completely flattened and others torn apart with untouched upstairs rooms leaning dangerously down toward the search parties.

At three in the afternoon they ate lunch at Red Cross headquarters, then started back to work. Marie and Hardin James were in a group with two teenage boys and a forty-three-year-old retired Marine sergeant who had been injured in the Gulf War. The sergeant had lost three fingers from his right hand and wore a strapped-on device that looked like something from a futuristic movie. He pulled apart wrecked houses like a madman. His name was Dooley Williams and he led his group with a fierceness and concentration that was amazing to watch.

At six o'clock in the evening they stopped at what had been the corner of a residential block. It was beginning to get too dark to see nails and glass on the ground. Thirty minutes before, they had found the bodies of two women and a twelve-year-old-boy in a house behind them. The firemen working the area had come in and cleared the area and removed the bodies.

"They were in the bathroom," Hardin said several times. "They were in the bathtub and they still got killed."

"You kids want to go back to the rest trailer?" the sergeant asked. "It's getting too dark to see." The sergeant was worried about Marie. She looked tired and she had started crying when the firemen came and removed the bodies.

The sergeant took a bottle of Gatorade out of his pocket and held it out to her. "Drink this," he said. "You don't want to get dehydrated."

Marie drank part of it and handed the rest to her brother.

"We have flashlights and there's still light in the sky," Hardin said. "Let's go through that bad block one more time."

"There was a baby stroller in that house with the bodies," Marie said. "There should be a baby, but there isn't a baby. Why would they have a baby stroller in the living room unless they had a baby? I'm a babysitter. No one keeps a baby stroller unless they have a baby. They take up too much room."

"There's no baby here," the sergeant said.

"There's no furniture either," Marie insisted. "Let's look one more time."

"Okay, one more hour, but let's collect the other kids from Fayetteville." He called the group behind them on his cell phone and the leader sent John Tucker, Jason Hall, and Tommie Anne Farley to join the sergeant's group.

"Marie and Hardin want to look one more hour. We're going to spread out and search as long as we can see. Does everyone have flashlights?" Everyone had them. John Tucker had two.

The sergeant called Red Cross headquarters and told them they were staying out another hour. "Volunteers numbers 26, 27, 28, 29, 30, and me, Sergeant Dooley Williams. Ten-four."

"Where do we start?" Hardin asked.

"At the first house on the block and work our way around the four sides. We didn't look all the way into the middle of the cul-de-sac because we found the bodies. Zigzag into the center when you can. Spread out."

Hardin had been walking alone through the debris for twenty minutes when he saw the piece of cloth. It looked like a colored square. He drew nearer and saw that it was a cloth doll in the shape of a giraffe. He picked it up. It was soaking wet like everything in the debris. He wrung it out, then stuffed it into the pocket of his jacket. He speeded up, stepping through the broken boards and nails and bricks and the long branches of a fallen oak tree. He pushed apart the branches and then he began to scream. "Over here, Marie, Sergeant Williams, a baby, it's a baby."

He reached down into the branches, which had fallen on a mattress, and picked up a big, fat baby boy dressed only in a diaper and a torn white shirt.

He picked up the child and held it against his denim jacket. He held it as close as he dared. Its eyes were open. It was breathing. A living, breathing baby boy in a soaking wet diaper. He kept holding it against his shoulder, only once moving it enough so he could be sure it was still breathing. Then Marie was there and Sergeant Williams right behind her. The others were moving toward them, coming from four directions.

The sergeant called the Red Cross trailer. While they waited for help they stood in a circle with their bodies around the child, barely able to speak in the wonder of their find.

"He isn't crying," Marie said. "He should be crying."

"He's in shock," the sergeant said. "He'll be okay. He's breathing. He'll be okay."

Marie pulled off her windbreaker and her blue Izod shirt and put the shirt on the baby and pulled off the soaking wet diaper and tied her windbreaker around the baby's legs.

John Tucker took off his football jersey and put it on Marie and they all moved closer to keep the baby warm.

"The wind blew him here," Tommie Anne said. "He flew here on the wind."

"Why isn't he hurt?" Marie said twice. "How did he land?"

"They're flexible," Sergeant Dooley Williams said. "Babies are real flexible from being curled up in the womb while their bones are growing." Marie had the baby now cuddled up in her arms in her blue Izod shirt and the windbreaker, cuddled up against John Tucker's Fayetteville High School football jersey. He was a running back. Hardin was a kicker. He kicked the field goals and he was very good at kicking them. He didn't know why he could kick them. He just could and he practiced hours a week to make sure he didn't lose the gift.

They all stood there in the brilliantly clean, rain-cooled and rain-scrubbed air, close around the baby, barely daring to talk about what was happening.

The baby began to cry. Sergeant Williams called the Red Cross again. "Get someone over here," he yelled into the phone. "We have a baby here. A living baby. Corner of Chestnut and something. You'll see us. You can see us."

The baby began to cry louder. Sergeant Williams pulled a cookie out of his pocket and broke off a piece and handed it to Marie to give the baby. "He's big enough to eat," he said. "I've got kids. I know about such things."

Police cars were arriving from three directions with their sirens running. Men were running toward them. A very large woman in a police uniform got there first and took the baby from Marie.

The baby's name was Rafael and his father was alive. His father had been at work on a night shift at a chicken-plucking plant in Dardanelle. The dead people in the house were the baby's mother and grandmother and older brother.

Rafael's father got to the Red Cross trailer twenty minutes after Marie and John Tucker and Jason and Hardin and Tommie Anne got there. He picked up his son and sat cuddling him in his arms, sitting on the edge of a straight chair.

"Theese is your shirt?" he asked Marie.

"It's his now," she answered. "I'm okay."

AT NINE THAT night the Fayetteville Five started driving back to Fayetteville. For a long time no one really talked. Then Marie began.

"Last spring when I met my biological father I told my mom, Annie, I thought nothing important would ever really happen to me again. She told me I was wrong."

"The stock market crashed," Jason said.

"That's nothing compared to this. This could be the most important thing that ever happens to any of us as long as we live."

"No, it's not," Hardin said. "Lots more is going to happen. I haven't even gotten my driver's license yet. All I have is a learner's permit."

"I almost didn't come with you," John Tucker said. "I only came so Tommie Anne wouldn't be driving my car."

THEY STOPPED AT a filling station in Carville and then drove across the street and got hamburgers and french fries at McDonald's. Marie went into the restroom and put on a T-shirt she had bought at the filling station. It was dark green and had some sort of corny painting on it but she wanted a clean shirt and it was the only one in a small.

"Wear it inside out," Tommie Anne suggested.

"And have this ugly painting next to my skin. No way."

Tommie Anne leaned in close and looked at the painting more closely. "What's it of, anyway?" she asked. "You can't even tell."

"It's some kind of monster truck from a video game. See, it says MONSTER MADNESS. Disgusting."

"How much did it cost?"

"Five ninety-five. It doesn't matter. We found a baby boy

alive in the ruins of a tornado. I'd wear this shirt to school to get to be there again when Hardin started yelling and we went there and saw it. I'm going to start liking Hardin a lot more after I saw him holding Rafael. Rafael—I'll remember him always. When he gets bigger we have to go to Adkins and see him and maybe take him to a park to play. I don't want to lose this night forever."

"We will. We'll go see him every year and see how he is doing."

"He lost his mother and his grandmother." Marie looked down. She didn't want to cry again. It embarrassed her to keep crying about things.

"And his big brother."

"That's another reason I'm going to start liking Hardin. I'm going to tell him I like him and not get mad if he wants to watch his stupid football games on television when I want to watch *Say Yes to the Dress*."

"*Say Yes to the Dress* is so good. I could watch it all day."

"Let's get out of this bathroom. We have to get on back home before our parents freak out. Dad's called four times."

The next morning the story was on the front page of the *Arkansas Gazette* along with a photograph of the baby's father holding the baby. In the photograph the baby was still wearing Marie's baby blue Izod that she liked so much she washed it by hand in cold water so it wouldn't fade. There was a quotation in the story about her putting it on the baby. Later that week she received a package from the manager of Dillard's Department Store with three new Izod shirts in her size. One baby blue, one yellow, and one white.

"How did they find out my size" was all she could think of to say when she told her friends about it.

"What did it feel like?" people kept asking Hardin. "When you picked it up and it was a baby?"

"Like a miracle or like if you hit a ball out of the field in the last inning of a championship game. But more than that. It felt like I'd never known what to think before and all of a sudden I knew exactly what to think. But mostly that he was breathing. You could hear this little, little noise of air coming out of his nose. Like we all do it every day but never listen to it. I don't know. I don't want to talk about it too much. I don't want to lose it all in words."

"YOU WERE STANDING there in that old pink bra?" Marie's mother said several times. "I don't believe you were just standing on the street in that grimy-looking pink bra."

"I got dressed in a hurry when we decided to go," Marie answered, getting irritated with her mother after she had sworn to stop getting irritated with her since it didn't make any difference to get mad. "The bra was on the floor where Ella throws her clothes when she takes them off. I put it on in a hurry. Listen, Mother, if I don't get a room of my own soon I am going crazy. I'd take that little room off the kitchen that used to be a pantry if I have to but I'm not living in a room with Ella anymore."

"I'll talk to your father tonight. We can build an addition if we want to. We can afford it. We've just been putting it off. I'll talk to him tonight. I'll see what I can do."

Her mother turned back to the stove where she was making Courtland stew, her husband's favorite food that his mother from Edinburgh, Scotland, had cooked every week. "I don't blame you for not wanting to have a room with Ella. So I'll try to get it changed. We are very proud of you, Marie. There are not many sixteen-year-old girls in the world that get to save the life of a baby."

"You save them every day, Momma," Marie said. "At the hospital. You do." She looked up at her momma and thought how much she forgot to tell her mother she was proud of her and swore to herself she would not be irritated by a thing her mother did ever again, even if she kept on making that stupid stew just to make her father happy.

Marie walked out of the kitchen and out into the living room where Hardin was getting ready to go to football practice. It was Saturday morning and it wasn't even football season and he still had to go out and practice kicking field goals with his football coach.

"Good luck with your field-goal kicking," Marie said as she passed through the room. She stopped to say some more, since it felt so good to have decided to be nice to everyone in her family. "I really like to watch you kick them. You get to make points all by yourself that win or lose a game while the rest of them have to run all over the place knocking each other down. I think it's great you can do it. So good luck with your practice." She smiled her kindest, nicest, not-acting-but-really-smiling smile.

Then she went out the door into the beautiful spring morning to walk down to the square and see if there was anyone else around she could be nice to. But not Ella, she decided, thinking of her older sister, asleep in their shared bedroom with her clothes all over the floor like the mess that was her mind.

The sky was a perfect brilliant blue like the brand-new Izod she was wearing above her cutoff jeans.

I'm lucky today, Marie decided, and stopped to inspect the brilliant yellow forsythia blooming all along Mrs. Collier's fence. I hope Rafael's doing all right. His father said he had two aunts who would help take care of him. I hope he has a good day today and doesn't know his mother isn't here.

God, I have to start being nice to Ella no matter how much I have to try to do it. She might be the only one left to take care of my baby, if I had one, and if a tornado came and killed Mother and Hardin and me.

Now that she had something really good to think about, Marie walked faster and moved down the hill from Duncan Street toward Center Street, thinking all about what it would be like after there was a big funeral and everyone in town was crying and the only ones left to take care of the baby were her father and Ella.

As she neared the square she ran into a teacher she used to have in the sixth grade, and the teacher started asking her all about the tornado in Adkins and what it felt like to be a hero, and Marie started telling her everything that had happened and added some more things she sort of made up.

"So I was in this Monster Truck Madness T-shirt, but I didn't even care. I'm going to give it to the Salvation Army, only I hate to fix it so some poor person has to wear anything that ugly. Maybe I'll just cut it up and make dust cloths out of it. What would you do?"

"Cut it up," her sweet, wonderful, chubby-faced, old sixth-grade teacher said. "Remember that thing I gave you all to read. 'Whatsoever things are good, whatsoever things are lovely, whatsoever things are of good report, think on those things.' "

"You're right. That shirt is the opposite of pure and good

and lovely. Thanks for teaching us that. You were the best teacher anyone ever had."

Marie hugged her old teacher and patted her on the head, noting that she was now taller than the darling lady who used to read wonderful things to the class every afternoon just when they got to the time when they were so tired of being at Root Elementary School they could die.

Well, what a week, what a month, what a year it was turning out to be, and summer coming soon, wonderful old summer with sandals and short shorts and swimming and, well, chiggers, if you forgot to use *OFF!*, and trips to take and maybe John Tucker finally realizing how much he liked her. After all, he had put that jersey on her after he saw her in her bra.

"I sure bet he didn't notice it was dirty," her best friend, Abby, told her ten or twenty times. "No guy would be noticing if a bra was dirty if he ever got to see one. You really didn't think about having it on and nothing else?"

"I was thinking about that baby being cold and wet. I was thinking exactly what somebody was supposed to think. It was a training bra anyway, something Ella used to wear to run in. It's really big, bigger than lots of tops or bathing suits girls wear all the time."

"Don't think about him thinking it was dirty. That's the last thing that was on his mind."

"We were thinking about the baby," Marie adored saying

every time she and Abby discussed the matter. "We were thinking about Rafael and nothing else. We had cut off our flashlights to save the batteries and it was almost completely dark where we were standing in the middle of the worst mess you could possibly imagine. Just standing there thinking about Rafael flying through the air and landing on a wet mattress with boards all around him. I remember it like it was a moment ago and I will remember it until I die. If I live to be a hundred like my great-great-grandmother that I'm named for, she was French, then Rafael will be about eighty-seven and maybe he'll come to my funeral."

"The stuff you think about, Marie. You ought to become a writer."

"No, I'm going to be a nurse like Momma, although she thinks I ought to go on and be a doctor. I might. What do you think?"

"I think John Tucker already knows he likes you. He just can't say it yet. How could he help it? You are the most interesting person anybody knows." Abby was tired of talking about Marie then, and started a conversation about herself.

They talked about Abby for a while, then went into the kitchen to see if they could find anything to eat.

They found some leftover Courtland stew and put it into a pan and added Cajun Seasoning Salt and butter and heated it and ate it with crackers.

"It's a Scots thing they eat in Edinburgh, Scotland," Marie

told her friend. "The reason there's always some left in the refrigerator is it's so tasteless. My dad likes it that way because it reminds him of his mother. My mother likes the smell of burned toast because it reminds her of her grandmother. Her grandmother read books all the time so she forgot to get the toast out of the oven until she smelled it burning. She'd scrape it off and eat it that way but she never made my mother eat it burned. She always ate it burned with the burned part scraped off and she still does it. They didn't have toasters back then when my grandmother cooked toast for my mother. They just had ovens and you had to watch things that were toasting.

"Think about the things old people have in their memories, just thousands and thousands of days and people they knew and stuff they did and you don't remember much of it. It has to be something like finding Rafael to make you remember what happened on a day long ago. Burning toast and your grandmother yelling and tearing open the oven and getting out the toast and scraping it off."

"Your mother ate it too? Did she get to like it?"

"She said her grandmother would cover up the burned part with a lot of butter and maybe homemade scuppernong jelly and that she liked it better than regular toast, what with all the excitement that went with it. I remember my mother's grandmother, but only when she was really old, not when she had a kitchen and burned the toast and all that."

"We'll never forget each other," Abby said. "We'll be friends forever even if one of us moves to California or Australia."

"We will," Marie answered and reached across the table and took her friend's hand. "How do you like the stew?"

"It's okay," Abby said. "I guess you could get used to it."

ON APRIL 4, 2009, the Fayetteville Five and John and Tommie Anne Farley's father, Caleb Farley, drove to Adkins to visit Rafael Fernandez and his aunts and father. They were driving in the Jeep Cherokee that had taken them there in April 2008. They were being followed by a Channel Five Television truck with a crew who were going to film the visit for a CBS special on the tornado and the recovery the town of Adkins was making with help from all over the state and the surrounding states too. Governor Beebe was there and Senator Blanche Lincoln and several state representatives.

The Fayetteville Five were being given citations for their work, which embarrassed them all except Marie who actually liked being on television. "It's because you're so photogenic," Tommie Anne told her. "You'd look good in the Monster Truck T-shirt."

"You look good also," Marie said. She meant it. Tommie Anne's mother had taken her to Pink Papaya the day before to have her hair done and had bought her some new Clinique makeup to replace the drugstore stuff she had been using. "Just for this special occasion," her mother warned her. "So make it last. If you want more you have to use your allowance or babysitting money."

THE MAIN THING was seeing Rafael, who was two and a half years old that week, and seemed very happy with his life. He was a smiling, laughing boy with green eyes and black hair and was left-handed, something Hardin was the first to notice since he was also left-handed. "The reason I can kick field goals is because I use my left foot," he told Rafael's father. "Also, it's a big advantage in baseball and in tennis."

"I know these things," Rafael's father said. "I am using left hand, too." Hardin and Mr. Fernandez laughed together, and Rafael moved in and started laughing with them. "He knows if something is funny very much," Mr. Fernandez said. "He is always laughing very much."

Hardin and Marie and John Farley and Jason and Tommie Anne played with Rafael for twenty minutes before Caleb Farley let the television crew come in and photograph them holding him and watching him walk around trying to touch all the camera equipment.

ON THE WAY home Marie sat in the second row of seats beside John Farley. He never had told her he liked her for a girlfriend or asked her for a date, and he was two years older than she was and getting ready to go to college. Still, she had not given up entirely on something happening between them someday. After all, she was one of the prettiest girls in Fayetteville so tell me he hadn't noticed.

"I wish you'd come by our house sometime and hang out or go for a walk with me. I go up to the university every afternoon and walk for at least an hour. It gets my mind clear for doing my homework and all that. I'm on this campaign to really like the members of my family and know how valuable they are to me." She had turned toward him and was making him look at her.

"I think anyone who was in Adkins on the day we found Rafael should always stay close friends, don't you," she added.

"Sure," he said. "I'll do that. I'll come walk with you one day. I have to get used to the campus since I'm going there in September. Do you know the names of different buildings up there?"

"I can find them out on my iPod," she said. "I'll start learning them when I'm up there."

She's going to talk to me all the way to Fayetteville, John Farley decided. Well, she is real pretty and she was there with us. She's right. We ought to keep in touch with each other.

"Good," she said now. She reached out and touched his hand and patted it for a minute, then took her hand back. "I'm going to consider that a promise. Any afternoon. I'll be waiting."

He wants me to shut up, she decided. I can quit talking if I want to. I've done it before. I'll do it again. I'll just be thinking about Little Rafael and when he gets big and we go to see him play baseball or tennis. I'll bet he's going to be a star. He's a star-quality baby if I ever saw one.

I need to remember all this. I don't want to forget sitting next to John Farley in the Jeep Cherokee right after we were all filmed for CBS News. I don't want all my memories lost in some fog like most people's are. I am capturing mine every chance I get.

Collateral

Carly Dixon was getting ready to go to class when the phone rang and she answered it. "Our unit's leaving tomorrow afternoon for Gulfport, Mississippi," her unit commander said. "Do what you have to do. We need every man and woman, Carly. This is what we trained for."

"All right," she answered. "What do I need to take? I'll need a letter for the college. Well, maybe not."

"There's a meeting this morning at B gate of the staging area in Springdale. At ten. If you can't make that, there's another one at six this afternoon in Fayetteville at the old basketball arena on the campus. People are dying down there, Carly."

"I know they are. Okay, I'll make the one this morning."

"Ten-four."

"Ten-four."

Carly took off the short red skirt and white cotton blouse she had been planning on wearing to teach her first Accounting II class at the University of Arkansas School of Business, a class she had been waiting to teach since she joined the faculty and the best job she had ever dreamed of having, and the first time anyone in her family had ever taught at a college or made fifty thousand dollars a year, but she still had to make extra money to pay off the hundred thousand dollars in loans it had taken to get her to the place where she could make fifty thousand dollars a year, so she took off the red skirt and put on the uniform of an Arkansas First Responder in the National Guard and got ready to go join her helicopter rescue unit at the hangar in Springdale where they trained every weekend. She had never gone down in the basket to pick up a wounded or helpless human being, but she had picked up plenty of her fellow first responders who were pretending to be helpless or wounded and she knew she was ready.

She was a triathlete who had run fifteen marathons and ran every afternoon for an hour and a half and worked out at the health club with weights in any spare time she had, which wasn't much as she was teaching two early-morning classes per semester, taking classes in the English Department for a secondary degree, raising her thirteen-year-old son alone and had a boyfriend if you could call an undependable thirty-year-old man who was still in college a boyfriend.

She finished putting on her uniform and went into the kitchen and got her son's breakfast ready. When he came into the kitchen she told him what was going on.

"I have to go to New Orleans to help save those people down there," she said. "I have to leave tomorrow. I don't know how long it will be. You have to stay with Grandmomma and Granddaddy. Can you do that, Daniel? Can you be my big man?"

"Yes, ma'am. That's good, Momma. I wish I could go. I'd like to see that."

"I'll take pictures if I can. Do you know how to download them if I take the digital camera?"

"I wanted it for the, well, never mind. That's more important. Will they pay you extra for doing this?"

"A lot, I think. That will be good, won't it? Hey, maybe when I get back you can have a camera, too. I'll get you something nice to pay you back for this."

"At least Granddaddy's house is close to school. I won't have to get driven every morning."

"Finish eating. Let's get going. What time is practice over this afternoon?"

"I'll call you and let you know." He stood up. He was getting tall. Tall and skinny like his daddy had been. And he was a man. No matter what else life had dealt her, it had given Carly a man for a son, and she did not forget to be glad about it.

They went out and got into her Honda and she drove him to school and let him off and then she went to the university to tell them she had to leave. "I e-mailed my students the class was canceled for today," she told her boss. "I have to go to this meeting."

"We'll be proud," the head of the department said. "I'll teach your classes myself. I wanted to send money down there but we're pretty strapped right now with both of our kids in school up north. This will make me feel good. Call when you can and let us know what's going on." He walked around the desk and gave the lovely, strong young woman a hug and meant every word he had said. "I'll get your schedule and see that the classes are met. You go on."

Carly left the business school and went next door to Kimpel Hall and put a note in the mailbox of her creative writing teacher, a woman younger than herself who was a student in the Master of Fine Arts program in fiction. "Dear Starr," the note said. "I've been called to go help my helicopter unit (National Guard First Responders) rescue people in New Orleans. Don't kick me out. I'll really have something to write about now, won't I? Yours sincerely, Carly Dixon (Creative Writing II, 3401, Room 302, Kimpel Hall)."

"BRING BEDROLLS AND everything you need," they were told that morning. "There's nowhere to buy anything and there are mosquitoes, so bring insect repellent. I'm not counting on supplies for a few days. We will be staying in tents in Mississippi. We'll do daily runs into New Orleans, then re-stage in Mississippi each night. Don't plan on having electricity. Our planes are bringing our supplies and water. I called Walmart and we are putting our tents near to where they are bringing emergency supplies, so if the government fails us we can always call on Walmart for backup. Questions?"

There were plenty of questions, most of which didn't have answers.

CARLY SPENT THE evening moving her son, Daniel, over to her parents' house and getting him settled. She had bought him a book of twenty-dollar Traveler's Checks from the Arvest bank. He knew how to use them from a trip they had taken the year before to Colorado. Carly had always been very careful to teach Daniel about money. She didn't want to give her parents money for him as they might be stingy with it.

"I'll come get you in the morning and take you to school," she told him when she left.

"You don't need to do that. It's only four blocks. I'll walk or take my bike."

"But I want to see you before I leave. I just think you ought to go on and spend the night here tonight because I have a lot to do."

"It's cool. Is Charlie coming over?"

"Yes."

"That's cool. Go on, Mom. I'm proud of you. I told my coach. He said he was jealous."

"I'll tell him whether to be jealous when I get back. They said there are swarms of mosquitoes and we're sleeping in tents and it's hot as hell. I may wish to God I'd never taken that National Guard money."

"No, you won't. It's an adventure. Go save some people."

"I might. I hope I will." She turned at the door and looked at him. Her man. Her thirteen-year-old chip in the future. It's hard to love someone this much, she decided, and went back into the room and hugged him again. She refused to think about his dead daddy. She just, by God, never thought about his dead daddy. His daddy was dead. That was it. His daddy had run a motorcycle into a tree on the Pig Trail when

Daniel was three years old. He had not been wearing a helmet and he was dead and they didn't find the body for a whole day and when they did they called her and she buried him and then she swore she wouldn't think about Dan being dead or think about him being alive because she was going to stay alive and make a life for his son and not be a mourner or a whiner as long as she was alive and she would stay alive.

SHE WENT OVER to the university track and ran six miles, then she went home and took a bath and put on her nightgown and waited for Charlie to come and spend the night. He was a waiter at a restaurant on Dickson Street and a student in engineering at the university. She had been seeing him for two years without deciding she wanted to get married again.

She waited for him in the darkened living room. She lit three small gold candles scented with pine and lavender. Then she went to the front window and stood in the dark waiting to see Charlie's car come down the street. It was ten after ten. He had said he was going to take off early so they could have the night together before she left.

At ten-thirty she gave up watching for him and went into her bedroom to check the bag she had packed. She turned on the overhead light and went over her supplies. She had tried to pack light, but she had to have moisturizer and sun block and bug spray and lipstick. She took her new Chanel lipstick out of the bag and put a cheap lip gloss in its place. She wasn't ruining a twenty-dollar lipstick when she was going to be living in a tent.

She sighed, trying to decide if three T-shirts were enough. The phone rang. It was Charlie.

"Where are you?" she asked, but it was a useless question. She could hear the music and the noise.

"At George's. Come on down and join us."

"I thought you were coming here."

"I was but Mick wanted me to have a beer with him first. Listen, the Cates are playing later. Come on down."

"I have to get up early. Besides, I'm not going to be around you when you're drinking. I've told you that."

"I met your writing teacher a minute ago," he said. "She was telling a bunch of people about you going off to save lives. She's real excited about it. She got your note."

"You met Starr?"

"She's here with her girlfriend. Come on down. All you have to do tomorrow is fly down there. She wants to talk to you about where you're going. I tried to fill her in."

"I'm hanging up, Charlie. I don't talk to people when they're drinking. That's it. Good-bye."

"Baby, calm down, would you?"

Carly hung up the telephone and went into the living

room and blew out the candles and put the safety bolt on the front door and turned out all the lights in the house and went into her bedroom and zipped up her duffel bag and threw it beside the door and checked her alarm clock and turned off the overhead light and climbed into her bed and turned on her meditation CD by Dr. Andrew Weil. She skipped the CD to "Guided Meditation with Sound," closed her eyes, and went to sleep.

SHE GOT UP the next morning and drove to Springdale for early morning drills and to listen to speeches about how they should conduct themselves in an emergency zone.

At noon she was back in Fayetteville and went by the junior high and took Daniel out to lunch at McDonald's. The school was nice about letting him leave for an hour.

Then she drove back to Springdale and parked the car and reported for duty. Her group of fourteen first responders flew on a National Guard plane to Jackson, Mississippi, where they picked up ten more helicopter crew members and then flew to the airport in Gulfport, Mississippi, where they were met by trucks that transported them to the site of the tent camp that was being constructed by a Coast Guard squadron from North Carolina.

"The newspapers are full of condemnation for the Guard," their commander told them at the first meeting that afternoon. "The newspapers are mad because we can't put together a rescue operation in less than twenty-four hours so I'm asking you not to listen to television or read newspapers for a few days because I don't want all of you to be as angry as I am. All we have to do is get into our groups and find our aircraft and start fulfilling our mission. There isn't time this afternoon to make a run but I want helicopters in the air before dawn tomorrow. I want everyone in bed by dark tonight. If you need sleeping pills there are medics to give them to you. Get sleep now because in the morning we are heading out. We have four copters and backup pilots. We have enough supplies for a week, thanks to the Alabama Guard, and we're on our way." He stood back and the technical people turned on the projectors and showed them aerial views of the area where they would be working in the morning. There were people on roofs. There were people screaming for help. It was chaos.

"We are going to save lives one at a time without putting our crews or equipment in danger," the commander said, stepping in front of the screen. "Remember that. You can not get in a hurry and do something right. We are going to save these people one person at a time, one roof at a time. Got it?"

"Yes," the teams said back at him.

When they got back to the tents Carly unrolled her bedroll onto her cot, took her cosmetic kit and walked to the prefabricated ladies room and washed her face and brushed her teeth and went back to her cot and debated for a minute whether to take the Ambien she had been given by the medic. She took fifty milligrams of Benadryl instead, getting ahead of the mosquitoes, and put on her pajamas behind the screen, said good night to the woman from Jackson who was in the cot beside hers, put a mask over her eyes, and went to sleep thinking about where she was and what she was there to do. You ought to be here with me, she said sleepily to her dead husband, Dan, breaking her vow not to think about him alive or dead. If you hadn't gone and killed yourself you would be here seeing this hurricane. Goddamn you to hell for getting yourself killed. I take that back. I just hate to think of everything you're missing. He's playing ball on the football field where you played when you were his age. You're missing that and you're missing this. Never mind. Om, mani, padme, hum. Om, mani, padme, hum.

It was a mantra Carly had learned in yoga class at the Fayetteville Athletic Club, where she worked out when she had time. One thing about the National Guard, they gave her better health insurance than she got at the university and they paid her health club dues, not that she ever used the health insurance, because her aunt was a registered nurse and if she wanted to know anything or get any antibiotics, she just called Aunt Roberta.

Om, mani, padme, hum. It was working. Now she was

thinking about Aunt Roberta instead of Dan and it was better, a lot better. Her Aunt Roberta helped Dr. Bill Harrison deliver babies. She had helped deliver hundreds and hundreds of babies. Her Aunt Roberta was the best-looking sixty-year-old woman in Fayetteville and had helped deliver half the people in town.

Carly fell asleep laughing at the thought of her Aunt Roberta up at the hospital being the first person to see the face of half the people in Fayetteville High School. Including me, Carly added in her sleep. She helped deliver me.

At four the next morning the tent full of first responders began to wake up and trudge to the restrooms and brush their teeth and put on their clothes and boots and collect their gear and march out to the staging area and collect into groups and head for their helicopters. By six a.m., they were over New Orleans. By six fifteen they had sent the first basket down to the first roof and brought up the first victim, a ten-year-old girl with legs as long as a zebra's legs and a smile as wide as the sky and Carly's heart lifted and she thought maybe she had lived her whole life to get to be the person that pulled that little girl up into the cockpit and undid her straps and handed her a package of Ritz Crackers with peanut butter and a bottle of Mountain Valley Water from Hot Springs, Arkansas. "You aren't allergic to peanuts, are you?" she remembered to ask.

"No, ma'am. I'm not allergic to anything. They going to get my momma and my grandmother?"

"We sure are, Honey. We'll have them in a few minutes. We have to circle back around. Was that all that were there? The three of you?"

"Yes, ma'am. Is this water green?" She was examining the green glass bottle.

"Honey, that's the best water in the world. When Bill Clinton was president of the United States they had that water in the White House in Washington, D.C. You want me to get the top off?"

"I can get it. I sure am glad you came to get us. We been scared to death up there."

"Eat those crackers. Drink the water. It's going to be all right." Carly reached over and patted the child's arm. She opened the package of crackers and held one out. I'm just like Aunt Roberta, she decided. This is like what she does. When I get back to school I'll make a poem out of that. I bet Starr will like it. I hope they don't kick me out of the class because I'm gone. Well, they won't.

CARLY WAS WRITING an e-mail to her son, Daniel. He had sent her one saying his history teacher wanted her to come talk to the class when she got back. "His name's Mr. Beebe and he's from down there where you are. He was in a hurricane named Betsy when he was a child and he remembers all about it. He wants to meet you, Momma. He isn't married."

"Dear Daniel," Carly wrote back. "Are you trying to fix me up with your history teacher? I'm glad to think you are thinking of me. It's unbelievable down here. I shouldn't tell this, I guess, but I have helped save a lot of lives. The first person we saved was a ten-year-old girl with long skinny legs and the best smile. We have to put the people we get off their roofs on an overpass over the drowned city, or else we put them out at the municipal airport. We are all trying not to watch television but just read things in the local newspaper which is printed as e-mail. We have some electricity at our camp. Our camp is a tent city. We have meals three times a day if we are here, and the rest of the time we eat the same meals they give troops in Iraq. Saturday night some people are going to barbecue for us. You can't believe how much it means to see people on their roofs and to be able to take them to a safer place. I think I will never forget this.

"I'll come talk to your class if you want me to. How are Grandmomma and Granddaddy? Give them a kiss for me and don't be any trouble but I know you won't be.

"Love, Momma"

At the Saturday-night barbecue all the rescue crews put on whatever regular clothes they had with them and tried to act like it was a normal party. They had tables set out on the deserted beach and the moon was full and the Gulf of Mexico looked like a normal place to have a picnic but everyone was so tired they mostly just ate the barbecue and mashed potatoes and went back to their tents and went to bed. Several days before, they had been issued mosquito netting and Carly was using hers religiously. She had used up all her bug spray in three days, and, although they had been promised new supplies by the Walmart reps, none had been delivered and Carly was starting to think she was going to be eaten alive.

What next, she decided. Well, hell, don't start thinking like a prima donna. This is the job and you are going to do it.

Her computer was beeping in its case underneath her cot. She pushed away the netting and rolled over and pulled it out from under the cot. She sat up and opened the case. The red light meaning "new messages had arrived" was on and she was curious to see who they were from. She had talked to Charlie briefly two days before, but Charlie never e-mailed her so it wouldn't be him. If there was trouble with Daniel her mother would have called her cell phone.

What the hell, she decided. Just open it and see.

It was from her old friend, Cynthia Jeans. "Dear Carly, We are all so proud of you here. I'm watching it all on television every morning and every night. Don't get in that water. That water is toxic. If you get in it, wash it off immediately.

"Here's the bad part. Charlie was down at Jose's the other night with this girl named Starr. I think she's in the writing program. She's from New York and wears see-thru blouses. Tacky, tacky, tacky. Then he was with her last night at George's and if it was me I'd want to know. I never have thought he was good enough for you anyway. He has gone out with every accomplished woman I know in this town and it never lasts. He's been in school for ten years. When is he going to graduate? He didn't like seeing me at George's and didn't introduce me. I found out from a man I know that's in the language department in Kimpel Hall who the girl is.

"I love you. I had to tell you this. I couldn't get you on your cell phone. What's wrong with it? Do you have electricity? Come home soon. Love, Cynthia."

CARLY FOUND HER last e-mail from Daniel and read it. Then she typed him a reply. "This is an amazing adventure. When I get home we are going down the Buffalo River, if we get any rain, or we are going down to see the Hogs play Ole Miss or something good. Start deciding what you want to do to celebrate — this work is so hard but so rewarding and I am going to deserve to go somewhere with you and have some real, even expensive, fun. Good luck with the team. Are you going to get the position you want? If not I'll yell at the coach when I get back. Just kidding, love, Momma."

THEN SHE SHUT off her computer, put it back under the bed, took one of the sleeping pills they'd given her, and lay back on her cot and put her arms beside her body, but that felt like a corpse so she put them folded over her flat, tight stomach, but that felt more like a corpse, and then she got tickled thinking about how relieved she would be not to have to talk to Charlie Ames anymore, ever.

THEY WERE UP at five the next morning, ate breakfast in the mess, where a new cook was making some really killer biscuits. It turned out he was a chef from the famous restaurant Commander's Palace who had refugeed to Gulfport and signed on as a cook to help the relief workers. He was the talk of the tent city after that first morning with the biscuits. He said he'd tried to copy the ones they make at Kentucky Fried Chicken, having figured out they were half butter. He told people he'd been sneaking out to eat those biscuits for twenty years. Carly ate two biscuits and scrambled eggs and grits, then climbed into the Big Huey that had arrived the day before from California, and flew off over the early morning mists to New Orleans to finish bringing out the people. There were small boats all over the flooded areas now. People with boats had come from all over to help save the stranded. "Sean Penn is down there. He's been here two days, going out," a woman in the cockpit said. "He used to be a lifeguard in California. They said on television he was working like a madman."

"Maybe we'll see him," Carly said. "He'll probably want our autographs."

There was gunfire going off near a house they were trying to fly to and the pilot turned and went out over the Gulf and called in to see what they should do.

"Abort and go to section seven," the dispatcher said. "Don't go near gunfire. Report it and the police will bring police boats."

"There are four people on the roof. None of them had guns."

"Abort it. Go to section seven. They have four houses to empty there."

They were using Carly constantly to go down in the basket to get children because she was so light that sometimes she could bring up two at a time. The first time she went down on this day she brought up a young girl with a baby. The second time she brought up a boy Daniel's age. She had tried to think about Charlie going out with her writing teacher, but it made her so mad she couldn't concentrate. Then it stopped making her mad. Then it made her furious, and finally, after she went down for the boy, it just made her feel superior. What a bunch of losers, she decided. Maybe I'll take Daniel and go live in Bentonville where they have people who are doing something for a living. Fayetteville has too many people who are just hanging out.

That night she had an e-mail from her boss at the business school telling her what he was doing with her classes and telling her she had been given a raise of 2.5 percent and the department had filled out the papers and put her up for tenure track. "We're all proud of you, Carly," the e-mail ended. "I hope you'll have lunch with me when you get back and give me a report. We're pulling for you. Don't get hurt."

"I DIDN'T GET quarterback," Daniel wrote to her. "John Tucker got it again, but I'm going to be a running back and catch his passes. I'm glad. It's because I'm tall, coach said. When are you coming home? Our first game is Thursday night, against Springdale. Love Daniel."

She thought about all the years she had put him out to play in the sand below the broad jump pit while she ran laps around the university track. After a while he always got bored and ran with her. So he's a running back, she

decided. Even without a father, thanks a lot, Dan, for running into a tree without a helmet. You stupid fool. I take it
back. Thanks for the genes.

AT THE END of their second week in the tents,
their commanding officer told them they were leaving on
Sunday night so to get packed up. "Turn in all your hours, in
flight, and on the ground. You'll be paid within the month.
Checks sent to your regular addresses. Make out forms if
addresses have changed."

CARLY SAT ON the edge of her cot and thought that
she was going to miss the tent and the cot and not having to
think about anything but getting in the chopper and going
to work and coming home and taking showers in the out-
door shower stalls and treating her bug bites with cortisone
and taking sleeping pills if she had the least bit of trouble
sleeping. Well, I'll get the real world lined up now, she decided. She called a friend who worked in registration at the
university and canceled her enrollment in the writing class
and signed up for a beginning class in conversational Spanish
instead. As a professor she could take a class for free every
semester.

She got the e-mail address of the Spanish teacher and
e-mailed her and told her the situation. "I had two years

of Spanish when I was an undergraduate," she explained. "I won't be any trouble. I'll just audit if you like. I'm good at speaking it. I just want to get better. I'll come by your office as soon as I get home and introduce myself. I hope you'll let me in the class this late."

Then she called Charlie and left him a message saying it was over. "I'm through," she said. "Please don't call me. I'll get someone to bring your canoe and anything else you left at my place to you. I mean it, don't call me. You don't want to hear what I have to say."

Good-byes on Sunday were emotional. Carly exchanged numbers with a dozen people she might never see again. Then she climbed into the big Huey and flew in it all the way to Springdale, Arkansas, as it was going to have to be ferried back to California by their unit.

She was met at the Springdale airport by her son and her father. "He's teaching me to drive," Daniel reported. "We've been going out to an old road near the lake. I can drive real good, Momma."

"Really well," she said. "So, Dad, is all that true?"

"He's a natural, Baby. Wait till you see him. He's careful."

Daniel picked up her duffel bag and threw it into the trunk of the car and she climbed into the backseat to let the men be in the front.

"When's the next game?" she asked.

"Thursday, at home. But you can come and see a practice if you want. My coach wants to meet you. Everyone knows what you've been doing, Mom." He turned around in the seat and smiled at her and Carly decided she might just be the luckiest person in the world and maybe she was going to keep on being lucky.

"A chef from one of the best restaurants in New Orleans was cooking for us the last week we were there," she said. "He said he's going to come up to Fayetteville and live until the mess down there gets cleaned up. He used to come up here to visit in the seventies. I'll take you out to eat if he gets the job he wants at the Thirty-Six Club. Wait until you taste his biscuits."

THEY DROVE INTO Fayetteville down the old Highway 71 that people still called College Avenue from a time when it had been a lovely street lined with huge maple and oak trees that led from the farms outside of town to the university. Now it was a strip of fast-food restaurants and car dealerships and beauty supply shops and chain drugstores.

"I'll be so glad to get home," Carly said. "I want to sleep in a bed. I feel like I've been to war. I really do. Every bone in my body hurts. The main thing I want to do is put on my shoes and run on some hills. I've been running on a torn-up highway beside a beach. I want to see some places where people aren't depressed and homeless."

"Well, here you are," her daddy said and turned off the highway and headed up Maple Street toward their neighborhoods. "If the global warming people are right, we may have a beach right here in Northwest Arkansas in a few thousand years."

"What have you been watching?" Carly asked.

"The Discovery Channel," Daniel said. "He watches it every night."

CARLY LIVED IN a small frame house painted blue. It had three bedrooms and a back porch that had been turned into a sunroom. The floors in the house were light-colored hardwood. It had taken Carly four years to finish fixing the house so that she loved to live there and so that Daniel could bring his friends home without being ashamed. There was a small yard with maple trees and a neglected flower garden. There was a front porch with a swing painted bright red and wicker chairs that had seen better days but always had fresh cushions as Carly's mother couldn't stop making things on her sewing machine even if you asked her to stop. There were pots of geraniums that had been pretty when Carly left to go to New Orleans but were full of yellow leaves now since no one had been there to pull them off.

Carly had bought the house with the death benefits she received after Dan Dixon's motorcycle ran into a tree on the old Pig Trail leading from Fayetteville to Alma. It was a narrow, winding road that for many years had been the quickest way to go to Little Rock. She owned the house free and clear and she loved the little house and spent a lot of time keeping it repaired and everything in working order.

It was on a small street seven blocks from the university and fifteen blocks from the junior high where Daniel was in school. It was only six blocks from Fayetteville High School. It was an old neighborhood on small hills that made it an interesting place to live when there was snow.

CARLY'S DAD LET Carly and Daniel off at their house and leaned on the steering wheel worrying about them. "You got everything you need?" he asked. "I bet there's nothing to eat. You want me to go to the grocery store for you?"

"We'll be fine. Go on, Dad. Thanks for coming to get me and thanks for taking care of Daniel."

"We don't want him to leave. I wish you'd give him to me."

"Shut up," she said, and kissed her father on the cheek and got out of the car.

"Call your mother tonight, honey. She wants to talk to you."

"Has she been talking to Cynthia? I broke up with Charlie. Has she heard that? Tell her, will you. I know she hated him.

Tell her I said she was right." Carly laughed and leaned on the car door.

"Your mother never hated anyone in her life."

"Okay." Carly kissed her father good-bye and followed her son into the house. The house had the musty smell that houses get when no one has been there. Daniel and Carly opened all the windows and turned on the air-conditioning fan. "I'll have to go to the grocery store," she said. "There's nothing here but stale milk. You want to go with me?"

"No, I'd better do some homework. Grandmother's been after me so much I'm about to get in the habit of wanting to do it."

"I broke up with Charlie. Are you glad?"

"I heard you tell Granddad. I'm glad if you're glad. Yes, I'm glad. I didn't want you to marry him. He tries too hard to get in good with me."

Carly put her arm around her son and hugged him to her. "You take care of things around here. I'm going to the store."

She drove down the street to the IGA and filled a basket with basic supplies and paid for them and started out the door. Three people she knew closed around her and asked questions about New Orleans. "You're a celebrity," one of them said. "Everyone in town is talking about you."

"That's all I need," she answered. "There goes my last refuge."

• • •

She woke at dawn the next morning and went out for a real run for the first time in weeks. Then she went back home and woke Daniel and made his breakfast and went into her closet and got out the red skirt she'd been meaning to wear to her first class. New beginning, she decided. New year, new ways of being, no drunks.

She got out her engagement calendar and started marking out the Thursday afternoons for Daniel's ball games. Then she packed her backpack and drove her son to the junior high school, then went to the university to learn and to teach.

Her classes were good, reasonably small, and so well trained by Dr. Williams in her absence that she wondered if she could live up to the standards he had set. No one was wearing a baseball cap, something she hated and felt badly about asking them not to do.

That afternoon she went by the junior high football field to watch Daniel's practice. When she took a seat in the stands he was already on the field, catching passes from his good friend, John Tucker, and looking so old it made her sad.

"Is that your kid?" A man her age had come to sit near her. He was tall and big-boned and powerful, the kind of man her father was, and she warmed to him at once.

"The one in the yellow shirt. He's my only child. I'm Carly Dixon. That's Daniel and that's John Tucker McCarthy throwing to him. He's the quarterback that was so good last year. Do you have a son out there?"

"I sure do. He's a seventh grader who kicks field goals. Well, he's trying out to kick field goals. He's a soccer player really. I hate for him to start football. I ruined my shoulder playing when I was in school. But you can't stop them, can you?"

"It's a lot different now. You'll be surprised. My brothers and my cousins were always getting hurt, but now they play shorter halves and the rules are stricter and the pads are better and there's a physician here at every practice."

"I hope you're right. See that little kid over there with the blue and white striped shirt. That's Jesse."

"With curly hair. Like yours."

"I'm Grady Clayton. My boy's Jesse." Grady Clayton climbed down two rows and sat beside her. Not too near, just on the same bench. "I'm about to fall asleep," he said. "I just got back from New Orleans. I drove all night because I took a wrong turn and went through Memphis."

"I just got home from there. Yesterday. I'm with the National Guard. I was there for two weeks. It's really awful, isn't it?"

"Not like anything I've ever seen. I'm trying to send some trucks down there to help with the cleanup, but I hate to send my men down there into that unless I can make it worth their while. What were you doing there?"

"I'm a first responder with the Guard. We do helicopter rescues."

"Wow," he said. "I'm talking to a heroine."

"No, I'm just a momma hoping my kid will get to start the game Thursday night."

"Is that what you do? You're in the National Guard?"

"I'm a college professor," she said, and giggled. Grady Clayton was a man who made women giggle. "I teach in the business school."

"Hell, I'm out of my league here," Grady moved in a little nearer.

The whole team had come out onto the field and the coach was talking to them. They moved into a circle, then spread out across the field in three groups. Daniel was in the group with John Tucker, so that meant he was going to play in the A group.

Grady's kid, Jesse, was down at the end of the field with an assistant coach getting ready to practice field goals. The coach set up the ball. Jesse kicked it expertly between the goal posts. Then he did it again with a second ball.

"That's amazing," Carly said to the boy's father.

"They came and pulled him off the soccer team and asked him to play. I hope I don't regret it." Jesse kicked a third football exactly between the posts.

"That's amazing coordination," Carly said.

"Yeah. Well, we'll see how he does when the wind's blowing and the pressure's on." Grady was trying to sound practical, but he was beaming. "I want to talk to you about New Orleans," he told her. "I need input. I'm fixing to lose a lot of money down there if this turns out to be a bad idea."

"What are you going to do?"

"I'm a trucker. I called down there last week and offered to send some trucks to help move some of the debris off the highways but they kept jacking me around about the contracts so finally I drove down there to see the problem. Their main highway along the coast is torn up. Well, you know if you've been flying over it. I'm sending fifty trucks down there on Thursday if I can get the men to drive them. I'm not letting a bunch of strangers drive my trucks. Look out there, Miss Carly. Your kid just made a great run."

"I taught him to run. I used to have to take him to the track when I'd do laps. At first, when he was little, he'd just play in the sand at the shot put, at the university track, then he started running with me, I guess because he was bored." She looked over at Grady and took in all his big shoulders and long legs and wide chest and she was about to think she was just a tramp forever when he smiled his wide, good smile and she just went on and let herself get interested. Except he's probably married, she decided. Well, no ring, but what does that mean anymore?

"I taught Jesse to kick," Grady said. "When I was in junior high I was small for my age so I kicked field goals to be on the varsity. I played for the team in seventh grade kicking balls and now there he is. His mother's pretty tall, I don't think he'll stay small but he might. He's tough though, real tough." He stopped, then looked right at her and went on. "I'm divorced from his mother. It's hard on him."

"Daniel's dad is dead," Carly answered. "Since he was three. But he has my dad and my brother. Life's harder than we know it might be when we're young. It's funny how it happens to you, isn't it? But when you see folks after a real disaster like in New Orleans it makes this look like nothing. I mean, regular messes like divorces or getting fat."

"Am I fat?"

"No." She giggled again. He kept doing that to her. "God, I didn't mean you are fat. Women, I mean. If I stopped running I'd get fat, but I'm not going to stop."

Four other parents had joined them. Then half a dozen more. A woman Carly knew came and sat by her and held out a bag of M&Ms. Carly ate a handful of them and passed the bag to Grady and he ate some, too.

"You're not fat," she said. "You're a big, good-looking man." She giggled again. Well, what the hell, she decided. So I'm interested.

Grady Clayton went home from the ballpark before the

practice was over but not before Carly left. A friend was bringing Daniel home. "My ex-wife's going to pick up Jesse," Grady said. "I don't like to run into her if I can help it. We just got divorced last year and it's still pretty raw between us."

"What happened?" Carly asked.

"Who knows? I thought she liked me, then she stopped."

"I'm sorry," Carly said.

"Well, I'm not, except for Jesse's sake. I have him two weekends a month. That's not much but, well, hell, I hate to get you into all that. She's not . . . well, you'll probably meet her this fall so I'll just say this, she's from up north and she doesn't understand the South. I'm surprised she's letting him play sports. If you make her mad she can really make you sorry so I don't want her to think she has to run into me all the time if he plays football."

"Sit on the other side when she's here. Tell Jesse where you'll be and why."

"That's good advice, Carly. Thanks for that. Hey, do you have a card or something in case I need to ask about things?"

"No, but I'll give you my number." She wrote her cellular phone number on a piece of paper and gave it to him. In return he fished around in his billfold and found a card and gave it to her. Clayton Engineering, it said. Long and Short Hauls, Gravel, Cement, Stone, Ornamental Stone, Limestone, Rocks, Surveys.

"Oh, no," she said. "The way I need a driveway, this will burn a hole in my pocket." She giggled again and they walked together to the parking lot and he got into a big Mercedes and she got into her Honda and they waved good-bye.

One door closes, Carly thought, and another one opens. How did I get so goddamn lucky? I better hurry or I won't have time to run before I cook supper.

GRADY BROUGHT HIS parents to the game on Thursday night. They sat on the fifty-yard line ten rows up from the running track that circled the high school field.

Carly arrived just as the game started. She'd been held up by a faculty meeting at the university, which was only a block away, so she had left her car in the university parking lot and walked from her office to the high school football field. The junior high games were always played on the high school field, which is why they were on Thursday nights. The high school team used the old university practice field on those afternoons. It was an old arrangement made in the 1960s and still honored by the university, the high school, and the junior high. Fayetteville was still a small town in 2005 although you'd never know it to read the statistics.

GRADY STOOD UP and waved to her and pointed to the seat he'd been saving with his Momma's coat. Carly giggled. Stop that, she told herself. You really have to stop doing that. She waved back and went up and took the seat. "This is my mom and my dad," he said to her. "Alice and Jo Fred. This is Carly, Mom. The woman I told you about who goes up in the helicopters."

"Hello," Alice Ann said.

"Hi, there," said Fred.

"Oh, hello," Carly said. Well, she thought, at least I stopped giggling.

"I got you some M&Ms," Grady said. "I decided they might be lucky."

"We need luck against Springdale," Carly said. "They bring eighteen-year-olds." They all laughed at that. It was an ancient joke in Fayetteville that Springdale altered birth certificates.

"They really used to," Grady said. "In my day I know they did."

"When did you play?" Carly asked.

"Nineteen seventy-six to seventy-nine," he answered.

"You knew my husband," Carly said. "Daniel Dixon, he played at Ramey and then here. He would have been a senior when you were a freshman."

"I knew I knew that name."

At the half, Springdale and Fayetteville were tied 7–7. Fayetteville's seventh point had been scored by Grady's son,

Jesse, and Grady was lit with pride. When the half came Grady and Carly walked down to the refreshment stand and Carly let him buy her a Diet Coke.

"I really need to talk to you about New Orleans," Grady said. "Can you get away for lunch tomorrow? Or dinner, or anytime you can?"

"Come by tonight after the game," she said. "Come sit on my porch for a while."

"Okay. I will. Tell me how to get there."

"Do you know where Sanger Street is, up near the university?"

"Sure. I've lived here all my life. I know where everything is in old Fayetteville."

"Okay, I live in the middle of the block, in a blue house. It's eight six four. There's a mailbox with a number but it's hard to see at night. Eight six four, Sanger Street. Call me if you can't find it. I ought to be home about forty minutes after the game. Daniel's going home with a friend."

"I'll be there. As soon as I take my folks home."

AN HOUR LATER Carly was sitting on her front steps with the lights on in the house behind her. She had taken the wilted geraniums around to the back and thrown them under a trampoline. She had swept off the swing and the porch and the steps and put a bottle of wine in the refrigerator and tied her best yellow cashmere sweater around her shoulders. "It's just a man whose child goes to school with mine," she muttered out loud to herself. Then she added, "No, it's not. It's a good-looking man who actually works for a living and makes me laugh. How often does that happen anymore? Well, never."

IT IS A strange thing to begin a new relationship when an old one was really bad. Carly's relationship with Charlie had been bad, but Grady's marriage had been worse. His ex-wife was trying to keep his child from him, telling Jesse that Grady was a bad man, never packing Jesse any decent clothes to wear when he went to stay with Grady, any mean-spirited thing she could think up she was doing.

"What a game," Carly called out as soon as Grady started up the path to the steps where she was sitting. "I still don't believe we won. No one beats Springdale. How do you think we did it?"

"Your son scored a touchdown and mine kicked two extra points is how we did it and I wish we could quit while we're ahead. Watching their games is twice as hard as playing."

"Do you want some wine?" she asked. "I put some in the refrigerator."

"No, I don't drink anymore. I quit for good five or six years ago. I got tired of having hangovers."

"How did you quit?"

"I went to a counselor for a while. Then I went to a few AA meetings. Then I just decided not to do it. It wasn't that hard really. It was making me fat. So you don't think I'm fat?"

"No, you are not fat."

"I lost fifteen pounds after I quit drinking. I was fat. I was fat for three or four years. It's humbling, being fat. It makes you feel really bad. I ought to start running again. When do you run?"

"In the early mornings. I leave here and run up to the campus and circle it and then go down to the track and finish there."

"They still let people run on the track?"

"They let me. I know Coach McDonald. I chaperoned the teams to some relays. He gave me a key."

"Goddamn, Carly. You're a star."

"I am not a star. Stop saying things like that. So do you want a Coke or a Diet Coke or some Sports Tea? Sports Tea is good if you've never had it. It has potassium and ginger and licorice. You want to try it?"

"Sure. I'll try it." He sat on the wooden steps where he had sat down beside her in the dark on the porch and Carly got up and went into the house and returned in a few minutes with a tray and glasses full of ice and a pitcher and a plate of cookies. She set it down between them and poured the tea.

"Where's Daniel?" Grady asked.

"He's gone to spend the night with John Tucker. They have a test tomorrow and they are going to study for it over there. They were so high over the game I don't know how they are going to study history."

"I'm high over the game. When I was in high school I think we beat Springdale one time. We beat them by one point at one homecoming and that was because their quarterback was sick."

The moon had come out from in between clouds and was very bright. It was cool and the moon was bright and they were both scared to death of how much they liked sitting on the porch steps drinking Sports Tea and having seen their children win a football game. It made Grady so nervous he ate four of Carly's homemade chocolate chip cookies before he stopped himself.

"What did you want to ask me about New Orleans?" Carly asked, but Grady couldn't for the life of him remember and had to make something up.

"I heard some men almost got blinded because someone threw gallons of Clorox into the water at one of the pumping stations that take the water back out into the Gulf. Did you know anything about that?"

"Yes, I know all about it. We had a lecture about it the next day. There were people down there doing things no one in the world would believe. After a while it quieted down but the first week it was chaos."

"I was only there two days and most of the time I was driving around wrecked neighborhoods or being taken to see places they want to use for landfill. They don't even know where they can take the stuff that needs picking up. I kept telling people they ought to take tractors and just pile it up behind the levees on the lake to use for second barriers. Why move all that wood and debris fifty miles up to farmland? Or why not burn some of it? Well, no one's in charge. That's the biggest problem. No one has the power to say what's going to happen next. I took a lawyer down there with me and he couldn't believe the contracts they were wanting me to sign. He said he wasn't even sure what the jurisdiction would be if something went wrong. Mostly, they can't promise who's going to pay for work."

"It's really good to talk to someone who's seen it. I'm about worn out from answering questions from everyone at school. They can't imagine it. Let's sit on the swing." Carly got up and then bent down to get the tray but Grady already had it and had moved it to a table near the porch swing. Carly sat on one side of the swing. Her white cotton skirt was soft and made of something that looked like a soft, soft sheet. When she sat in the moonlight on the swing, the material fit down against her legs and draped along her knees and Grady was glad it was dark when he sat down across from her on a chair.

"I'm not saying anything," he said at last. "I mean, I don't want to say anything you think is wrong. But I want you to go out with me and soon. I want to be with you. Is that okay to say, Carly Dixon? Is that going to make you mad at me?"

"I want to make love to you," she answered. "So does that make you mad? But not now, it's too soon and you'll think I'm some sort of easy chick or promiscuous and I'm not and I never have been. But Daniel's gone to spend the night and we're both here. I don't know. What would happen if we went inside?"

"We could take a chance," he said. "I might have forgotten how. It's been awhile. It's been two months at least."

"Do you have a rubber?"

"I might have one in the car. Or I'll go get one."

"Then go look," she said. "I'll be inside. In my bedroom."

"I don't know where that is."

"Then I'll wait here for you."

In a few minutes Grady came back up on the porch. "I found something," he said. "I wouldn't swear it's much good. It's probably been in that glove compartment for several years."

"Come inside," Carly said and took his arm and led him into her darkened house and through the living room and into her bedroom where a small lamp was burning on a bedside table. "The bathroom is over there," she said, and pointed to a door. Then she unbuttoned the white cotton skirt and let it fall to the floor and she stepped over it and kicked it out of the way. Then she began to unbutton the blouse and Grady gave up being shy or scared because he had never desired anyone in his life as much as he desired this beautiful, talented, brave woman who was standing before him.

"I've never had any reason to have to use a rubber except to keep from making babies," he told her as he moved into her space and began to remove the blouse for her.

"Neither have I," she answered. "And I take birth control pills so get rid of it. We have a lot more to be afraid of than things like that, I think."

He picked her up in his arms and lay her down upon the bed and then he took off his clothes and lay down beside her and began to remember the heaven that men and women could sometimes give to one another, on certain nights, under certain circumstances, when the moon is right and the universe has decided to bestow its riches.

• • •

FIVE THURSDAY NIGHTS later, after Fayetteville won another game 7–6 over Bentonville, at Bentonville, when the children were settled and the cold night air had driven Carly and Grady into the living room where they were pretending to watch a television show until Daniel went to sleep, Grady picked up the channel changer and turned off the television show and very awkwardly turned to Carly and handed her a diamond engagement ring he had picked up from a jeweler at four that afternoon.

"If you will have me," he said. "If you will be my wife, I will love you and care for you and for Daniel until the day you die. Please say yes."

"What would we tell the kids? What if they don't want us to?"

"They will want it. We're good people, Carly. They love us and we love them. We'll work it out. I already asked Jesse anyway. I told him I wanted to marry you and he said it was good, a good idea. Well, he asked where we'd live and I said wherever you wanted to live and he said we ought to get a new house that was big enough for everyone. He said we ought to build one next summer when he was out of school and could help build it."

"Yes," Carly said. "I mean yes. I mean I want to be your wife, because I love you and I love Jesse and I think I could do this, but I have to ask Daniel. He has to be part of this."

"You think he's asleep?"

"No, he's too excited after games to go to sleep. He e-mails people for a while or calls his girl, you know, he's a kid, he's excited. They won."

"May I ask him, not any big decision, just ask if he'll think about letting me ask you to marry me?"

"Now? Tonight?"

"Yes." He hung his head way down into his chest, then lifted it and looked at her. "He's a man, Carly. I'll talk to him like a man. If he's hesitant we'll wait until I win him over. I think I can make him like the idea. Maybe I can't. He's always had you to himself."

"All right. You can try. I'll leave the house. I'll walk around the block."

She got up and went down the hall to Daniel's room and knocked on the door. "Come in," he said. He was on the computer writing an e-mail to his friend John Tucker. He finished the sentence, hit send and turned around to her, in all his thirteen-year-old-covered-with-victory glory he looked at her and it was as though he already knew what she was going to say.

"Could you come in the living room a minute and let Grady talk to you about something?" she said. "Something about us, about you and me and him."

"Sure," he said and he got up from the chair and stood beside her. "So are you guys in love or what? Is that it?"

"Yes. Do you mind?"

"I don't know. It depends on what you do about it."

He followed her down the hall to the living room and stood beside the sofa. Grady got up and faced him. "I'm leaving," Carly said. "I'm going to run around the block a couple of times." She went out the door and left them to it. She went down her sidewalk and out onto the deserted street and started running. One, two, three, four, five, six, seven, eight, she counted. It's all right. It's whatever it is. One, two, three, four, five, six, seven, eight.

"I WANT TO marry your mother," Grady said. They were both still standing. "I think she's the nicest lady I've ever met in my life. I wouldn't blame you if you didn't want to share her or live with us and Jesse or have to help us plan where we want to live. I would build us a big house or live here and add on to this house to make it bigger. I'll do whatever you want to do. I won't change your life, but I'd love to be your father to any extent you want that to happen. I think I'm a good one. I think Jesse will tell you that I'm fair and if I get committed I stay committed.

"What do you think, Daniel? It's up to you. Your mother said it's going to be up to you and you don't have to decide on this tonight or this month. I love Carly. That's not going to change. I waited all my life for her. I'm here on whatever terms I can get."

He stood there waiting and the thirteen-year-old boy, still wearing his football jersey but with pajama bottoms on beneath it moved nearer to him and put out his hand. "You can marry her if she wants to," Daniel said. "I love a girl. I know how hard it is. As long as you are always good to her and know she is the best. She's the best. I know that every day."

"You've made me a happy man, Daniel. I'll pay you back for your trust in me. I'll be the best stepfather I can learn how to be and you'll have to help me with that. So where do you think we should live?"

"Wherever she wants. I'd like a new house. Or we can fix up this one. I don't care. Houses aren't all that much to me."

Carly came in the front door and saw them laughing and went to her son and put her arm around him. "You said yes?" she asked. She was sweaty from running and her hair was curled around her head and her face was glowing. "You'd let me marry this guy?"

"I'd like to have a dad," he said, getting serious. "And I'd like to have a little brother as fine as Jesse. And I don't care where I live. Live anyplace you want as long as it's in Fayetteville."

They stood in a circle for a moment, no one knowing what to do next and then they moved into the kitchen and Grady started eating cookies and Daniel got out ice cream and started making chocolate milkshakes and Carly kept saying I have to comb my hair. Finally she went into her bedroom and put on a robe and combed her hair and Daniel poured the milkshakes into the glasses and handed one to Grady and they started talking about the ball game and the tight spot in the fourth quarter when Bentonville had the ball on the Fayetteville fourteen-yard line and Waylon intercepted a pass and Jesse kicked his tenth successful field goal of the season from the nineteen-yard line twenty feet from the center of the field and it made an arc and dropped behind the goal posts. "You should have seen it from the field," Daniel said. "It was like an angel was holding it. I wish he was with us now. It's not right he's not here for this."

"I told him I was going to ask you all," Grady said. "Before too long I'll get him for longer and more often. I've got a lawyer working on it. We're going to make it real expensive for his mother to be so mean. She stands in her driveway looking at her watch when I take him back on Sundays. I can't be a minute late. But if she wants to change my days she just does it and sends me word."

"You'll get him more," Daniel said. "I bet you will. He had a good time with us last weekend. He told me about the stuff she does to keep him from seeing you. He's not going to put up with that forever."

"What are you all talking about?" Carly asked. She had

come back into the kitchen wearing a blue wool bathrobe and with her hair combed and her makeup fixed. "What's going on?"

"We're talking about Jesse," Daniel said. "You want a milkshake, Momma? I can make you one."

"I want to see my engagement ring again," she said to Grady. "You put it back in your pocket. Give it here."

Grady took the box out of his pocket and stood up and handed it to her. "You don't have to keep it if you don't like it," he said. "Mr. Mozer said you can trade it for anything you wanted."

Carly took the ring out of the box and put it on her finger and sat down at the table and looked at her son. "I do want a chocolate milkshake," she said. "And I want you to make it for me."

In New Orleans, Louisiana, a beautiful little ten-year-old girl got up from her prayers and climbed into her bed in the trailer she and her mother and her grand-mother were using for a house. She had been praying the same prayers she had prayed each night for a month. She thanked God for all his blessings, for the new trailer and for cleaning up Lusher School and getting it started again. She prayed for her mother to get in a better mood and she prayed for her best friend, Sallie, and she said a special prayer for the woman with curly hair who had come down from the helicopter in the little chair and pulled her up into the seat beside her and strapped her in and told her not to be afraid. "Get her something nice that she really wants," Celia asked God. "Get her a new car or a new boyfriend or some pretty clothes or anything she needs. She's from Arkansas, but you know which one she is. She's the one who pulled Mother and Grandmother and me off the roof in the flood. I don't think you made the flood. I think you didn't know the canal barriers were going to break. Anyway, good night now, God. Amen."

High Water

So Dean Reyes and I had been in the French Quarter for five days and we weren't ready to leave. We work for a living and this was our vacation. Well, it was also a paramedics convention and our expenses were being paid by the hospital and the rest was tax deductible; still it was a vacation. We're paramedics in Los Angeles, a city so beset by AIDS and Hepatitis C and gunfire and every problem you can think of from an emergency worker's point of view that our hospital demands its workers take vacations. Anxiety becomes your middle name when you do the work we do.

What can I say to justify the decisions we made from the twenty-fifth of August 2005 until we got home on the six-teenth of September? We're only human. As Douglas Adams wrote, "In other words, carbon-based, bipedal life forms descended from apes." Only apes would have run from a storm, not decided to ride it out in the oldest apartment building in the United States.

Dean and I live together, but we are just friends, not com-mitted to anything as foolish as monogamy. We're proud of each other and we like the way we look and we like to be to-gether and we'd been looking forward to our New Orleans trip for months. We had three weeks of hard-earned vaca-tion saved and we weren't in the mood to have it cut short by a hurricane. We had wardrobes, connections, cash, and we weren't finished in New Orleans yet. We were shopping for antiques to tone down Dean's minimalist tendencies. We have a town house in the canyon and we've been redoing it all year.

We had driven to New Orleans so we could bring things home. We rented a red 2006 GMC Envoy and drove through Arizona, New Mexico, and Texas and on down to New Or-leans, "The City that Care Forgot." Let the good times roll, we had decided. We're ready.

So we weren't finished having fun yet and we didn't evacuate. So kill me. Mea culpa. Dean's an insomniac. You can talk him into anything if you don't wake him up in the morning on his time off.

We DIDN'T EVACUATE because WE DIDN'T WANT TO. Dean was sleeping until noon every day and I was power flirting with a tall, good-looking native New Orleanian, and besides it's the nature of our jobs to run toward natural disasters and not give in to fear.

We'd been having the best, best time and we'd both been super careful. Well, Dean was careful and I wasn't doing anything, as usual. I wasn't sticking my thing into any strange places without blood tests first when there was plenty of fun to be had power flirting, shopping, sashaying down Bourbon and Royal Streets, eating oysters Rockefeller and pompano meunière and drinking white German wines and French reds.

We'd gone to Antoine's twice in two days, once for lunch, once for dinner. And to Galatoire's three times. And to every other good restaurant in town. We found an oyster place called Casamento's that I'll put up against any in the world.

I was power flirting with a man named Charles Foret, who was a bit player in *The Runaway Jury,* besides being the only living male heir to an old New Orleans coffee fortune.

Then Charles invited us to stay with him for the hurricane and we did. "The Pontalba is the oldest apartment building in the United States," he told us. "Stay with me until it goes by. It will turn east. They always do."

We had barely shown our faces at the paramedical convention. Just went by the first day and got our credentials and listened to half of a boring speech about epidemiology and left our phone number at the hotel with a woman who was supposed to be our group commander.

Places we shopped that may never open again include A Gallery for Fine Photography, Harbison and Hunt Antiques of Royal Street, Boots and Belts, Your Grannie's Chairs, and Britannia Bed and Bath. God forbid I should ever think about the walnut and blue velvet chair that was in the back of the GMC when it was hotwired and stolen. The sales slip was in the glove compartment, Dean's idea. I will have the canceled check for the insurance but who knows how that will turn out.

STANDING IN LINE outside of Galatoire's is where I first met Charles Foret. Like he's the most elegant man I've ever seen this side of Durham, North Carolina. Tall, tall, tall and dressed in an unlined white summer suit with a pale blue tie he had made to match one described in a William Faulkner novel. "It's a copy of the tie V. K. Ratliff was given by the Russian woman after he may or may not have made love to her in the back of her shop in New York

City. It's my lucky tie. I knew if I wore it today something good would happen."

That's one thing I'll always remember about Charles. The other thing was after the hurricane, when we were alone on the levee watching a ship come down the river and he told me, ". . . Only one ship is seeking us. A black-sailed unfamiliar. In its wake, no billows breed and break . . . Philip Larkin . . ."

Charles has a PhD in English literature from the University of Virginia and has published poetry all over the world. Plus, he plays piano and paints and he thinks the world is good and for some reason he likes me. Plus he has a law degree.

"Standing in line at eleven forty-five in the morning is patently absurd" is the first thing he said to me. We were behind him in the line to Galatoire's, a restaurant that does not take reservations for anyone except the president of the United States. "I swear I won't do it anymore but here I am. Everyone comes here on Friday. I'm Charles Foret." He extended his hand and I took it. It was powerful and soft with long fingers and he let the handshake linger, didn't just stick out his hand and pull it right back.

"We're from Los Angeles," I said. "I'm David Haver. This is Dean Reyes. We came for the paramedical convention but we're playing hooky. Why won't they take reservations here?"

"A new way to be snotty in the world's snottiest town, with the possible exception of Charleston, South Carolina."

"I've never been in South Carolina. My parents are Lutherans from Minnesota. They don't take children to visit the South."

"I was in Charleston once," Dean puts in. "I liked it very much. Those squares are so beautiful. I really liked them."

A white-coated black man with beautiful gray and black hair came out the door and ushered Charles into the restaurant. He was followed by a younger waiter who took Dean and me around crowded tables and to the back where I could just make out the back of Charles bending over a table to kiss an older woman on the forehead.

"Was that an apparition?" I asked.

"I imagine so," Dean answered. "What do you want to drink?"

IT WAS NOT my imagination that made me think Charles was looking at me the whole time he was in the restaurant, and certainly not my imagination that saw and returned a long, wonderful smile right before he went out the door. Dean and I were deep into trout almandine and deep fried potatoes and a Piesporter Goldtröpfchen but I still caught that smile.

• • •

On Saturday Charles was in line again at Casamento's, the oyster place I told you about earlier. This line was even longer as the mayor was calling for evacuations and half the restaurants in town were already closed. Casamento's was serving until two.

"Hello, again," Charles said. He was with an older man he introduced as his cousin.

"Hello, indeed," I answered.

"Has your visit been good?"

"Except for this hurricane business. Do we really have to leave?"

"I'm going to my house in Mandeville," the cousin said. "I never stay for these things. If the electricity goes off it's a mess in this heat. You should leave this afternoon if you're leaving."

"I never leave," Charles said. "I live in the Pontalba on Jackson Square. It's right inside the tallest levee on the river. It's completely safe."

"Don't be a fool," the older man said. "I can't believe you'd take that chance." They argued all the way into the restaurant and to their table. Casamento's is walled with blue and white Italian tiles and it isn't that big. I could hear the cousin's voice until we were seated two tables away from them. All the while Charles was looking at me with his eyebrows raised in the most seductive and beautiful way. Dean was laughing at me. Adventure, imagination, exaltation, storm: we bipedal, carbon-based life forms know a good thing when we see it, and strangely enough I had no desire to copulate with the man. I wanted to talk to him for days and days and days.

I got to, it turned out, but not about literature and music and painting and plays or the state of the world or politics and history.

Waiters and waitresses were going by carrying trays of the most divine fried oysters and softshell crabs and oysters on the half shell, and people all around us were mixing ketchup with horseradish and squeezing lemons and drinking iced tea and digging in. A Force Five hurricane was bearing down upon the city but Casamento's was open until two and carbon-based life forms must be fed.

We were still eating seafood gumbo and buttered French bread when Charles came over to our table and invited us again. "I'm going to ride it out," he said. "It's too late to get on the highways. Please come and stay with me. I have enough provisions for twenty people. I hate to be alone with all this happening. We might be able to help other people when it's over. I worked in a hospital when I was young. I know how to do all sorts of things that might come in handy."

"We should," I said, and looked at Dean to see what he was thinking.

"Then we will," he said. "How do we get to your place?"

Charles drew us a map on the place mat and wrote down numbers and the address. "I'm going home as soon as I get Fanning on his way to Mandeville. Come as soon as you can."

So at three that afternoon Dean and I packed a few things in a small bag, called the convention center and left word of where we could be reached, put messages on all our phones with Charles's apartment telephone number, picked up our bag and walked out of the Royal Sonesta and down Royal Street past shops being boarded up and on down to Jackson Square, which was full of artists packing up their easels into old vans and starting to leave the city.

"I'm exhilarated," Dean said. "Haven't felt that in a while."

"This could be a mistake," I answered. "But thanks for letting me have this. I've been too good for too long. Listen, are we going to call our parents?"

"I'll call my brother in Ohio and tell him to call mine. I am not getting into this with my mother."

"I left a message last night when I knew they were already asleep. That's it for me. I told them we were going up to Mississippi. I always lie to them. I never lie to anyone in the world but my parents."

"Is that it?" Dean asked. We had come to a tall brick

building across from Jackson Square that really is the oldest apartment building in the United States. It is an amazing structure, ancient, almost Roman, built of handmade brick and stone, very solid and dug in. It is across the street from the Café du Monde where they make the famous New Orleans beignets and is behind a levee as high as its second floor. We went in through wide wooden doors and up two flights of stairs to Charles's apartment. He met us at the door and giggled with delight.

"Ah, company," he said. "I hate to be alone."

The apartment was floored with white polished oak. In the center of the living room was the most expensive black leather sofa I've ever seen in my life and two black Mies van der Rohe chairs and a marble table. So minimalist even Dean wouldn't find a thing to remove. There were black-and-white photographs by Ansel Adams, Cartier-Bresson, Karsh, Yavno, Edward Steichen, Clarence White, and Clarence Laughlin.

"It's a gallery," Dean declared. "My God, this is the best museum in town."

"My uncle Angus started it. I impoverished myself for the rest. Do you know Clarence Laughlin's work? He lived in an apartment across from here."

We toured the apartment and Dean was given the largest guest room and I was given one that shares a bath with Charles.

WE HAD BARELY settled in and opened wine when the doorbell rang and Charles' ex-mother-in-law comes in carrying a suitcase and a briefcase full of papers.

"Janet," he said. "This is a surprise. Why didn't you leave with Elizabeth?"

"I survived the cold war. I suppose I can make it through a television hurricane crisis. I tried to call but you didn't answer."

"Well, well, sorry."

"The police made me leave the house. They forced me to leave."

"Where is Elizabeth?"

"Gone to Baton Rouge. I wouldn't go." So she settles down on a sofa, not even acknowledging my or Dean's presence in the room.

"Mother Janet worked for MI-5 during the cold war," Charles said. "She did research in their legal department."

"I'll go to my room then," she announces and marches out to the room Dean had been given and lies down on the bed and starts watching news on the television set.

"Well," Charles said. "This is unexpected."

"Is she going to stay?" Dean asks.

"I'm afraid so. My divorce isn't final although we've been separated for two years. I can't be rude to Mother Janet. She is taciturn because she worked for thirty years with spies. I think we're stuck with her."

"Well, we can't make her leave unless we all do," Dean said. "The mayor is calling for mandatory evacuations as of an hour ago, whatever that means."

"We're safe here," Charles said. "We really are. Do either of you play chess?"

"I play," Dean answered, and they both laughed and got out the chess set and started a game.

AFTER A WHILE I went to the door of Janet's room and asked if I could remove our suitcase and she said all right and I picked it up and carried it out the door.

"What is she doing in there?" Charles asked.

"Watching television and reading legal papers she has spread out all over your damask bedspread."

"She likes lawsuits. She and Elizabeth have accused me of everything in the book, battery, infidelity, drug use. None of it is true and my lawyer gets it thrown out of court but it's cost me a lot of money. I can't believe she's here. I can't believe I have to nurse Janet."

"Ill-mannered people always manage to keep attention on themselves," I said. "They are like characters in a Pinter play. The meaner they are the more we think about them. I did a psychology workshop last year on people like that. It's a form of narcissism but even more destructive. Fascinating really. Well, if we can't kick her out I guess we just study her. If she goes to sleep we can steal her papers and read them."

"What's the daughter like? Your soon-to-be ex-wife."

"Like the mother only prettier. It was the great mistake of my life but I survived it and I got away."

"How did you get involved with them?"

"A blind date. Then she thought she was pregnant so I married her. I almost never do women. It had been a strange night in many ways.

"Then Mother Janet came from England and moved in with us because her house in London had been condemned."

Janet came into the living room as he was finishing this speech. "What is there to eat?" she said and went immediately into the kitchen and opened the refrigerator door and stood looking in.

"Don't leave the door open long, Mother Janet," Charles said. "We may lose electricity when the storm hits."

She took out cheese and bread and milk and started making herself a sandwich without asking if anyone else wanted anything. She put it on a plate and walked back into the bedroom.

BY TEN THAT night the storm had started to be fierce outside the windows. At midnight the electricity went off. At two o'clock Charles and Dean and I gave up trying to sleep and sat in the living room listening to the battery-operated radio.

Dean has a scientific mind. He was the first one to say he thought the city would flood. "Even if it lands to the east the tidal surge will come here," he kept saying.

"We're safe here," Charles kept insisting. "That's the tallest levee on the Mississippi River. That levee will hold. That levee is a hundred feet deep."

By four a.m. the wind was howling like a band of vampires.

"Coming for to carry me home," Charles kept saying for a joke but no one was laughing when he said it. Mother Janet got up from her bed and came into the living room and took up a corner of the sofa for a while.

"Are you all right?" I asked her several times but she didn't answer.

"Are you all right?" Charles added. Still no word from inside the mind of Mother Janet.

Dean got up and made a plate of crackers and grapes and cheese and handed it to her and she said "thank you" to him, which made us all feel better somehow.

When she finished the plate of food she got up and went back to her bedroom. "Call me when it's over," she said, and went back to reading her legal papers by the light of the only working flashlight that we had.

By six a.m. we decided the worst was over. The eye of the

storm had turned east and hit the Mississippi coast at Bay Saint Louis. We thought New Orleans had dodged a bullet.

IN THE EARLY morning as soon as there was light we went out into Jackson Square to look at the damage. A few neighborhood people were wandering around the square. Television cameramen were taking photographs of a statue of Jesus that had survived trees falling all around it. A wrought-iron fence was lying on its side beneath a live oak and signs were blown away and slate tiles were missing from historical roofs, but it didn't seem all that bad. The strangest thing was the smell, which I can only describe as unhealthy, not the clear, cool smell right before dawn you usually get for an hour in tropical cities after a rain but a smell of danger somehow, as though the storm hadn't really passed.

The other thing was how empty everything seemed, how quiet and deprived almost of oxygen.

Charles and I climbed the levee on the concrete steps behind the Café du Monde and that's when he told me the Philip Larkin poem about only one ship is seeking us.

"Too dark for me this early in the morning" was all I said. It was too late for romance to blossom any further between Charles and me. I was falling back in love with my old friend, Dean. He had beaten Charles at chess, three games

out of three, and his scientific mind had called the hurricane correctly all night long and now he was the one who
was saying the city was going to flood from the lakeside.
He didn't climb the levee with us because he was talking to
a television crew from CNN and had met a man who told
him the levees on the lake were already spilling water into
an industrial canal and it was going to be hell to pay before
the day was over.

Charles and I came down off the levee and Charles gave
the television crew a sound bite about how long his family
had lived in the Cabildo and then the three of us went back
to the apartment and had cereal and cold bread and then
Dean called the Tulane Medical Center and asked them if
they needed help. At noon we all went over there and pre-
sented our credentials and went to work. Charles went with
us because anything was better than staying in the Cabildo
with Janet, who was eating everything in the house and letting all the refrigeration out of the refrigerator no matter
how many times we asked her not to do it.

"Leave her to heaven," Charles said and went with us to
the Tulane Medical Center to lend a hand.

Here is what we found when we got there. A major teaching hospital with no electricity or water, generators failing,
water rising in the street outside its door, a staff who had
been up all night, and a team of doctors and nurses who

should receive medals of honor. We put on scrubs and went to work.

"Is this still going to count as vacation when we get back?" I kept asking.

"Probably," Dean said. "Don't talk, David. Just help me move these beds. We have to get these patients to higher floors so we can medevac them when they bring the helicopters."

Except, as everyone knows, the helicopters didn't come for two more days and when they came there weren't enough of them and the hospital next door had to send their patients to Tulane on rowboats including people who were dying and women with babies only hours old and so many other things I could not tell it all if I wrote all night. I'll say this for Charles. He dug in and did the work. He carried forty people up six flights of stairs in the dark. He slept on the roof when he slept and he got eaten alive by mosquitoes which is the main reason we broke into the Walgreen's on our way back to the Cabildo later the second night. We wanted to get a change of clothes and some food and we wanted Cortisone cream for the bites. We were in Charles's pirogue which a man who works for his family had brought to the hospital for us to use for patients. A pirogue is a flat-bottomed boat used for duck hunting in the bayous. We paddled the pirogue to dry land and then pulled it up on a sidewalk and looked around for a place to store it until we got back from the apartment. It was night but there was a moon and we had one flashlight we had borrowed from the hospital.

There it was before us. A drugstore, an almost new Walgreen's that had opened in the French Quarter a year before. "I didn't know there was a drugstore so near," Charles said. "I say we go in and get supplies. I say we replenish the hospital's supplies. I say we get me some insect repellant and cortisone cream."

"I say yes," Dean answered and before I could voice a vote Charles and Dean had dragged the pirogue across the dry street and were battering the Walgreens windows with the paddles. When that didn't break a window they grabbed the pirogue and turned the sharp end toward the window and rammed it through. We went inside and headed straight for the drugs. Dean used to run the pharmacy at the hospital and we knew what to get and where to get it. I went to the hardware section and brought back some tools.

An hour later we were headed back to the hospital wearing new clothes and carrying a boatload of sterile needles, tetanus vaccine, antibiotics, pain killers, muscle relaxants, antihistamines, sterile bandages, first-aid kits, and two ice chests full of ice, plus a case of bottled water. Dean and I were paddling, Charles was sitting in the prow putting flashlight batteries into flashlights and guarding the drugs so they didn't get wet.

Needless to say we were greeted as heroes by the staff at the Tulane Medical Center and sent back for more. We made two more trips before we were forced to desist by the presence of several policemen and about forty men and women helping themselves to the rest of the supplies in the store.

Dean's cousin, who is dean of the University of Nevada School of Law, says there is no way we can be prosecuted even if the police figure out we're the ones who broke the windows. He said he will represent us himself if they try.

Other things we took include reading glasses for workers who were struggling to read patients' charts while we carried them to the roof, boxes of diapers and formula for children, and several boxes of Hershey bars with almonds.

During the emergency I lost ten pounds, Dean lost seven pounds, and Charles is so elated by his service to mankind that he is thinking about going back to practicing law. "Think of the lawsuits," he said. "It will take twenty years to begin to settle with the insurance companies. I'll represent both sides. Maybe I'll become a judge."

It's the sixteenth of September and Dean and I are back in Los Angeles. Momma Janet messed up everything in Charles's apartment but she is gone now. Her daughter, Elizabeth, came in a van from Baton Rouge and took her away right before Dean and I left.

I asked Dean to marry me on the flight home but he said it was too much trouble and we could just go on living together if I didn't mind.

"We have wills and living wills and we live in Los Angeles," he said. "We do not need a marriage ceremony out of some ancient old religious book to make our friendship safe or sacred." He reached over and gave my arm a long, smooth, loving touch and then he put his first-class airline seat (we'd been bumped up by a gay American Airlines steward we'd met at a party in Sausalito last year) back as far as it would go and went immediately to sleep. For an insomniac he can sleep in the daytime more soundly than any human being I've ever seen in my life. His mother got his days and nights mixed up when he used to stay backstage while she was in Little Theatre plays in San Francisco.

What did I learn from my trip to New Orleans? Nothing I didn't already know except that we people are more powerful and quick on our feet than we know and can dig in and get it done if we have to. Also, everyone in the United States has too much stuff. We could survive these disasters a lot better if we all went minimalist. So there's no point in thinking about that 1950s walnut-and-blue velvet chair in the back of that red 2006 GMC Envoy. Leave that to the insurance adjustors. I'm back in California where all I have to do is wait for an earthquake and get on the internet and tell hurricane stories to our friends.

We saw some strange and wonderful things. We saw helicopter rescues and met television crews and watched Mother Janet ruin Charles's damask bedspread while plotting her daughter's divorce action to steal his property. Some people are heroes and some plot, some lie and cheat and steal, and some carry morbidly obese patients up six flights of stairs so they can be medevaced to hospitals and kept alive to eat another day.

The human race. You have to love it and wish it well and not preach or think you have any reason to think you are better than anyone else. Amen. Good-bye. Peace . . .

Toccata and Fugue in D Minor

It was April nineteenth, the second day of our journey to Italy. There were three of us, old friends come together to spend two weeks in a villa in Tuscany. Cynthia and Mary Jane were more excited about all this than I was as they had traveled less and were less weary of the process. Stuck all day in Heathrow Airport in the middle of a terrorist scare had proven who was right about that, but, strangely enough, it was me who kept on being cheerful and hopeful. Cynthia, whose wealthy husband had paid for the villa and the first-class British Airways tickets, was the first to become despondent. She had left two small children with a nanny to have this escape and there we were, in the midst of a bomb scare and a terrorist threat.

Nothing's ever lost on a writer, I told myself although I'm not sure I can call myself a writer. I make documentary films for the Public Broadcasting Services. I write the scripts, not that what I write ends up being what the narrators end up saying. By the time the language police and the lawyers get finished with a script, there's not much left. Anyway, nothing's ever lost on me, I told myself. I'll use this someday, whereas three women going to Tuscany to rebond has been done ad nauseam in recent years, which is probably where Cynthia and Mary Jane got the idea to begin with.

The beginning of the trip had been perfect, a private jet to Atlanta, then a luxurious journey across the Atlantic with a British Airways hostess to steer us through customs and into the first-class lounge at Heathrow. We got in at nine a.m. Our flight to Pisa was scheduled to leave at eleven-thirty.

We stowed our carry-on luggage with an attendant in the lounge, then wandered out into the shopping mall to get some exercise. I tried to buy a bright green leather handbag but Mary Jane wouldn't let me. "Italy is the World Series of leather shopping," she said. "Don't buy anything here."

"You can buy it on the way home if you don't find something better," Cynthia said. "We'll be here four hours on our way home."

"I've been with you one day and you're taking me over," I said. "It's because you have children and I don't have any. Your maternal instincts are sharp and honed. I'm going to be mothered. That's clear."

"We're sorry," they said together, turning to me. It was exactly like the old days at the Tri-Delt house at Vanderbilt. I was the one who needed roping in, Cynthia was the conciliator, and Mary Jane was the president of everything and arbiter of taste and manners.

"I want to buy that bag," I insisted. "I might not have time to look for one in Tuscany. I'm going to Italy to look at art, for God's sake, not to shop."

"Let her buy it," Cynthia said.

"It costs a hundred pounds," Mary Jane said. "That's a hundred and fifty-five dollars."

"Now I don't even want it," I said. "You have ruined the green leather bag for me."

"All right," Mary Jane said. "Let's go back to the lounge and get ready to go to Pisa."

"To the walled city of Lucca and Michelangelo and Leonardo da Vinci and Galileo Galilei and the Grotto Del Buontalenti, the Villa Garzoni and Giotto's Campanile," I chanted.

"The Giotto Campanile," Mary Jane repeated. She pronounced the name elegantly although twenty years of elocution lessons had never really erased her childhood lisp. It was a lovely fault in an otherwise perfect façade. "A sweet disorder in the dress," as the poet said, and certainly Mary Jane had had her share of powerful men. In the past ten years she had divorced a judge and married a vice-president of General Motors. She wasn't as wealthy as Cynthia was but she was doing all right.

"I want to really explore Tuscany," I said. "Five times I've been in Italy on business and I've never seen the Tuscan hills. It's the price I pay for working for a living. No wonder I don't like to fly, although that first-class flight on British Airways may make me change my mind."

We were collecting our carry-on bags from the desk when the announcements began to come over the intercom system. At first it was just flight times and cancellations. Ten minutes later the airport was locked down and nobody was going anywhere, not even out of the first-class lounge. Amid a buzz of cellular phones I called an editor I knew at the BBC and was told London was under siege. "I have to get off the telephone, darling," he said. "Be of good cheer. You'll be fine. It's just a terrorist threat. Stay calm."

Cynthia was staying calm. Her father had been a Republican senator from Oklahoma and she had things to live up to. Mary Jane was pretending to stay calm but the lisp was becoming more pronounced. "Let's just sit down," she kept repeating. Mary Jane was an attorney although she hadn't practiced in several years. She hadn't practiced since she divorced the judge, moving on to greener fields. "Let's sit down. Let's just sit down and let the people who know how to deal with this deal with it. Let's find a place — how about that big round table with the sofa behind it — and just settle in. This may take awhile."

"Go on over there and stake a claim," I said. "I'm going to use my press cards to see if I can find out anything."

"It's a waste of time," Mary Jane said. "The last person they're going to talk to is an American journalist."

"You're right," I said and we marched over to the corner table and put down our carry-on bags and set up a cozy spot to wait out the scare.

An American woman in pink slacks approached our table. "Could I sit here with you?" she asked. "They won't tell us anything. Did you see all the police in the place? Look out there." She pointed out the wide windows where the concourse was filling with uniformed men.

"Look that way," said a tall, older man who was listening from a nearby table. He got up and walked our way. "Look at the runways." Outside the back windows we could see our airplane surrounded by soldiers. Jeeps were bringing more.

"That's our plane," I said. "It's our plane that was targeted!"

I turned to look out the back windows. "They're all over the plane. We'll never get our luggage back. I guess you know that."

"Are you someone important?" the pink-slacked woman asked. She had stationed herself by my side. "You look like you know what's going on."

"She's Louise Hand," Cynthia answered. "She writes documentaries for PBS. And she used to write for *Vogue*."

"Cynthia," Mary Jane said. "My God. Louise doesn't want you saying who she is."

"It's all right." I turned to the pink-slacked woman and held out my hand. "Louise Hand, from Raleigh, North Carolina."

"Rivers Royals from Jackson, Mississippi," she said. "I'm on my way to Florence to borrow paintings for our museum. You really think we won't get our luggage back?"

"Not anytime soon. You don't want it if there's a bomb on the plane. It could be biological. We can buy more clothes."

"I packed my papers, for the museums. I had surgery on my hand last month and I can't carry things."

A British Airways attendant approached our group, which had grown to seven people. "We need people to stay calm," he said. "We'll get information to you as soon as we have it. There is tea and sandwiches, fruit and crackers and of course the bar, but we'd rather no one was drinking quite yet, so that will be closed for a while. We all need to keep our heads, don't you know."

I looked at Rivers Royals. She was trying not to smile. "Okay," I said, speaking for my group. "We're good. We've settled down. Don't worry about this corner of the room."

"I'm going for snacks," Mary Jane said. "I'll bring crackers and cheese." She stood up. "Anyone want to help?"

A man in a tweed suit stood up beside her and the two of them walked off toward the serving tables. The rest of us turned back to watching the soldiers search the airplane. They had turned dogs loose on the luggage, which was being hurled to the ground. Each piece came flying out the compartment door and landed in a pile.

"There's my bag!" Rivers said. "I put red ribbons on it. See the one the German shepherd's sniffing." We all watched. "I guess it's the computer," she added. "It has floor plans of all the museums in Florence."

"That might interest them." The tall man had moved nearer to us and taken a chair by Rivers. "Charles Halliday, from Memphis. You're with a museum in Jackson? I'm on the board of a museum, several actually. One in Ocean Springs, Mississippi, and one in Kansas City. Tell me about your work."

Rivers crossed her legs and composed her face and did a reversal now that there was a man for an audience. She straightened her back and moved her shoulders down. "We're doing a show of Italian masters. We want, I know this sounds crazy, to have a copy made of the David. Not life-size, of course, smaller, but not small. I have to get permission and talk to them about money. We have a backer, plus the state will help if we get it started. We would want to keep it for a permanent exhibit, of course, so that may cost more. It's all such a business anymore, isn't it."

Cynthia stood up and walked to the window. "There's my suitcase," she said. "I bought a cheap one so I could throw it away if the airlines ruined it. Prophetic. *They threw it out of the compartment!* If they think a suitcase has a plastic bomb, why are they throwing them on the ground like that?"

"They're in a hurry," I answered. "They have hundreds of planes to search with God knows how many bags. Sit down, Cynthia. It will only make you crazy to watch them search the luggage."

Rivers was continuing her story. "I studied art in Paris and Florence when I was in school. Then I got married and had children and my husband runs Mississippi Power and Light and he's busy so I have time to help with the museum. We are making quite a success of it. Did you happen to come to the Russian show last year? We made money on it. Actually, we made a lot, enough to help with these new plans. So what do all of you think about all of this mess? This terrorist thing and the war in Afghanistan and who should be our next president. I want to know what other people think. I really do."

"Oh, please," Mary Jane put in. "I'm going to sit at another table if we have to talk about politics or war. I really am. I will not listen to people give their opinions about politicians while we are sitting here in the absolute middle, the ground zero, if you will, of what the Muslim fundamentalists are doing to the Western world, which my ancestors helped create and which I am ready to fight to protect. I won't listen to it because sooner or later I'll have to hear someone spouting liberal hogwash and bashing the government of the United States of which I am a tax-paying citizen and of which I am proud." Mary Jane had stood up. Everyone had turned from the windows and was listening to her.

"Then let's tell the stories of our lives," the tall man named Charles Halliday suggested. "Stranded travelers are supposed to tell one another stories of who they are and how they came to the place where they are stranded. Shall I begin?"

"Oh, yes," I said, and everyone drew near and began to pay attention.

"My mother was from Kentucky," he began. "Her parents and grandparents all lived in a small town called Franklin and my grandfather was the editor of the newspaper there.

When I was in high school I played basketball and worked in the afternoon at the paper. I married the homecoming queen, later, when the two of us were seniors in college at the University of Kentucky. We were sweethearts from the time we were fifteen years old until she died last year of cancer. It happened very quickly. It began in her lungs and spread all over her body and nobody could save her. We used to smoke but had quit ten years before she died. I keep wondering if I'm next. For a while I wanted to be next, but now I'm better and want to live as fully as possible and see my grandchildren come into their full maturity. There are six of them. We had two sons. They are both married and work in my law firm but the younger one is leaving to work in Washington if his candidate wins the election. I won't say which candidate since you don't want to talk about it. All right, that's my story so far. I am going to the Italian Open and plan to stay through Wimbledon. I am a tennis player and my doubles partner and his wife will join me in Europe in two weeks. I have learned to cook, not much, but a little. And I am taking pleasure in my wife's garden which will be a mess when I return to the United States in August. My name is Charles Halliday as I told you earlier but my friends call me Charlie. Next."

"Mary Jane Tolliver, née Smythe," Mary Jane began. "I play tennis but not very well and mostly doubles. Lately I'm more interested in Pilates and yoga. I love to exercise. I've done it all my life. I don't do it to look good but to feel good and because I have a lot of energy I have to expend. Louise was my roommate my freshman year at Vanderbilt and we've been friends ever since. Cynthia is our other best friend. We were Tri-Delts at Vandy. We all got married and went our separate ways but we have kept up with each other. We used to meet each spring in New York City and go shopping and see plays. Then Louise got too busy and Cynthia and I are involved in our children's and husbands' lives and we sort of lost each other, so Cynthia thought up our going together to Italy to become friends again. I mean we are always friends but we don't really know our *new* selves, the ones we are now, but then, when we are together we are just the old selves again. Isn't that right, Louise?"

"Exactly right," I answered. "We revert to our old selves and it feels good, like finding an old shirt and putting it on and it still fits and you can't believe you haven't worn it in so long. I have to be tough in my working life. I have to make decisions and stick to them and be up and drink coffee and be on guard. Ever since yesterday I've felt like I was really on a holiday and all we have done so far is fly on airplanes and sleep while crossing the Atlantic Ocean and wake at dawn and land at Heathrow just in time to be locked down in a terrorist threat. What else about me? My family is an old Southern family and my aunt was a famous writer who committed suicide because she had cancer and didn't want to be treated for it. The treatments were worse twenty years ago. She walked into the ocean, in Maine, wearing a fur-lined Valentino jacket and leather boots. Anyway, that's the legend. We don't know what she was wearing because they never found the body. What else? The rest of the family are quite sane although some of them drink too much but some have quit, thank God. The thing I like about Muslim funda-mentalists is they want everyone to quit drinking. I hate al-cohol and almost never drink it myself. I think it has ruined our culture. Alcohol and sugar. I am thirty-five years old and I have never married but I want to be married. I just never can find anyone I want to live with for the rest of my life."

"I went to Vanderbilt," Rivers Royals said. "My God, I can't believe this. We all went to Vandy. I was a cheerleader there from 1975 to 1978. Then I quit because I married my boyfriend and moved home to Jackson. I never have finished college although I'm on the board at Millsaps College. I have four children, all grown. One boy, three girls. The oldest girl doesn't like me. She's a hippie vegetarian in Colorado. She's a big girl. She blames that on me. She says I fed her too many potato chips and wasn't at home when she came home from school in the afternoons, which is not true, but she believes it."

"Did you?" Mary Jane moved in closer. "Give her potato chips I mean?"

"No," Rivers answered. "The maid gave them to her. I was being in plays at New Stage Theatre but they would never give me the good roles so I quit that and started painting. Then I threw pots. I had a kiln, then I just decided to do good works and help the museum and the ballet. Jackson has an internationally famous ballet competition every spring. Nureyev came the first year and came back the year before his death. It's really a famous ballet competition."

"I should have guessed you'd been an actress," I said. "I love actresses. I'm fascinated by ego and the will to power."

"You want to talk about ungrateful children," the man in the tweed suit said. "I could tell you stories all day about that. I have a son who isn't speaking to me right now because I won't give him money. I sent him to school and graduate school. Well, I made him take out loans for graduate school but his father-in-law paid the loans for him. And I have lent him money to live on every time he quits a job he doesn't like. But finally I had to cut him off so he quit talking to me. He thinks I owe him a living but I don't. It's my fault this situation exists because I should never have given him money to begin with, much less all the money I gave him, but at least I stopped doing it. Better late than never. I'm sorry he quit talking to me but in another way I don't care. If it takes bad feelings to cut apron strings so be it. I read once that friends are the way God makes up to people for their families. My name is James, James Monroe."

"Tell me about your children," I said. "Let's trash our families. That will pass the time, and make me feel better about being childless. I'll trash the drunks in my family. There're lots of them and they're legends."

"The most interesting of my children is my oldest daughter," Cynthia began. "She's four years old and she would eat chocolate pudding all day if I let her do it. She is so much like my mother-in-law it scares me. She looks like my husband and she acts like my mother-in-law. I love her but I have to try to civilize her. Then my mother-in-law comes over and gives her anything she wants and plots against me with her."

"Plots against you?" Rivers asked.

"You wouldn't believe the things she tells her. She tells her not to pay attention to me and she favors her. I have a younger daughter but she isn't interested in her, only in Sophia, a name she conned me into naming her. I swear some days I think I have a cuckoo bird in my nest. That's what happens when you breed with people. You make some babies that are like you and some you don't recognize."

We were interrupted by a British Airways attendant. He was accompanied by a uniformed guard. "We need to see

Mrs. Royals a moment," the agent said. "If you would come with us."

"I'll go along," Mary Jane said. "I'm Mrs. Royals's attorney."

"And me," I added. "I'm her friend."

"Thank you," Rivers said. "Thanks so much."

The agent and guard seemed to have no problem with us going along so the three of us left the table and went into a room behind the information desk. It was a spacious office with computers and copiers and looked like an office in a brokerage firm.

"We need to unlock your bags," the guard began. "Would you give us the combination? We'd hate to break the locks."

"How did they get locked? I certainly didn't lock them. They were searched at the airport when I left Atlanta. Well, it probably happened when you threw them off the plane. The combination is four, four, four. I always use that. It's easy to remember. You have to clear it to the left first. Wait. I may have the instructions." She began to rummage around in her bag.

"No need for that. Just wait here. This won't take long I'm sure." The agent left and hurried out the door.

"Can I get you anything?" the attendant asked.

"No, thank you. We've had tea," I answered, then turned to Rivers. "Never a dull moment here on Planet Earth."

"I just figured something out," she said. "You must be

related to Anna Hand. She's my favorite author, lifetime. I cried all day when I heard she'd died."

"She was my aunt. My mother is her youngest sister. 'Louise, the selfish one.'" I hung my head. As always when a fan mentioned Anna I went into protective mode. Protect Anna, protect the family, protect myself.

"I'm sorry. I shouldn't have said anything. I know it killed you all. It killed me. I'm sorry."

"It's all right. It's been eighteen years. It never seems to go away, however, because of the books. How does it go: 'Power from the preceding generations hobbles the new generation.' I always think of that. Besides Anna, there is my mother. She's a noted journalist with three books. I keep thinking I should change my name to avoid comparisons, but it always seems too late. Mother kept her maiden name and after her divorce I took it, too. Because I'm proud of the heritage, proud of them." I was surprised at myself. I never opened up like this to strangers, especially not to Anna's fans.

"That line's from the epigraph to *Field Notes*. I always loved it too," Royals said. "'These are the patterns that enthrall a genetic line. Power from the preceding generations hobbles the new generation. Are we doomed to repeat the patterns?'

"My father was the Speaker of the Mississippi House of Representatives," she continued. "My mother is a doctor. They're a shadow and they're both in good health and still cooking. Thinking about me every minute. They'll know about this lockdown by now." As if on cue her cellular telephone started ringing. She didn't answer it. "It's probably on CNN that Heathrow's closed. They always know my travel schedules. They ferret it out of me."

"Go on and answer it and tell them you're all right."

"No. They need to get a life. All they do is read and watch television and spy on my brother and me. They try to get him to spy on me but he never tells them anything. He's a good man. You don't need a husband, do you? I'm looking for a wife for him. He's not wealthy wealthy, but he's got several million. He's a lawyer. He plays golf."

"I'll meet him if he's as interesting as you are."

"I'm not interesting. I'm a cliché inside a self-fulfilling prophecy inside a stereotype. I just let it happen. I don't fight it. I'm too busy being alive. How long does it take them to open my suitcase and find the computer?"

"Maybe they want to copy your files."

"That would be a thrill for someone. Nasty self-pitying notes from my large self-pitying daughter. Dumb fundraising ideas from my so-called peers in the Jackson Junior League, I get about sixty requests for money on any given week. The number increases every year. Carlton and I are thinking of stopping giving money to everyone for a while just to get some peace."

The agent returned. "We need to ask you a few questions," he said. "If you will go with me we need to go to another office. Sorry for all the bother."

"If you have my suitcase in the next room I'd like to get a few things out of it," Rivers began. "My hand is in a cast as you can see and there are things I need for it."

"How long do you think we are going to be delayed?" I added. "If there's been an announcement we didn't hear it."

"Please follow me," the agent said. "This won't take long. I'm sure there'll be an update soon on the situation." We all stood up and began to follow him across the long room full of computers and desks. Rivers was walking beside the agent. I was right behind them. "I can't imagine what you need to ask me about," she was saying. "If there's something in my suitcase I didn't put it there. I'm the wife of a powerful and influential man and I have lawyers. I want to call one of them and I want to know what's going on. I don't like this secrecy."

"They don't tell us what is happening," the agent said. "They just tell us what to do. Has anyone handled your bags since you packed them?"

"How would I know? My maid packed them. She's been my maid for ten years. She doesn't know what a terrorist is. I was busy getting ready to leave and in meetings to talk about the work I came to Italy to do." Rivers was starting to look angry and she was definitely turning into the star of the show. A sleeper charismatic, I decided. They don't call them upper-middle-class white protestant princesses for nothing.

We entered a larger office and sat in comfortable chairs while a British officer in a splendid uniform talked to us.

"What is your work here?" he asked Rivers.

"Not here in London. I'm going to Florence, Italy, to arrange to borrow some pieces of art, paintings, and to copy a statue by Michelangelo. It's for an exhibition we're having next year to coincide with the International Ballet Competition we have in Jackson, Mississippi, every spring. I'm trying to borrow two drawings by Leonardo da Vinci. You can imagine the time and trouble that takes. Not to mention copying the statue. We want to have the copy made in Italy. It's very complicated."

"Are there photographs on the computer of things you are trying to borrow?"

"And of fifty other works of art I'm going to see and talk about using. Plus all the financial information about borrowing them. You can call the museum in Jackson or my husband or any of my lawyers or the museum's lawyers or the headquarters of the ballet competition, or you can call the governor of Mississippi or our senators. Call the governor. His name is Haley Barbour and he's a friend of mine. He used to be head of the Republican Party but you aren't an American so maybe you don't know what that is."

"All right. I think that pretty much explains it. They said you wanted to get things from the suitcase. Could you tell me what you want and we'll have someone find them for you?"

"I want a change of underwear. Some panties and a brassiere. Tell them I want white ones. Not the colored ones, just some plain white underpants, you call them drawers, don't you, and a bra." Rivers stood up. "And if we're going to be here long I'd like my laptop computer when you're finished copying the files. . . ." He started to speak but she interrupted him. "Don't apologize. I want security to be tight. I don't mind being questioned. I don't mind having you go through my things. I am a grown woman. I should have known better than to travel to Europe during these troubled times but it seemed it would be worth it because art is a good cause or at least it used to be."

"We'll have someone bring your undergarments and the computer to you in the lounge." The panties and bra were getting to him. I could tell. Rivers was at least fifty years old but she still had the stuff. Not just the aforementioned slow-charging charisma but plenty of the sexual power that always accompanies it. She had these enormous and really lovely breasts and a small waist. Women with big breasts hardly ever realize the power they wield, even on men who weren't breastfed as babies. Anyway, I decided, the world is rich and full and everything keeps happening.

When we got back to the lounge our group was waiting for us and had grown. A young Chinese woman and her mother had joined us, and so had a tall, good-looking, redheaded man who I recognized. His name was Robert McArthurs, he was the book editor for the *London Telegraph,* and he had been my aunt Anna Hand's editor at Faber and Faber when they were young. I learned he had come across the room to see what the excitement was, and when he found out I was traveling with the group, he had waited to speak to me. I had met him years ago when he came to Charlotte to look at some manuscripts my Aunt Helen had found in Anna's papers. The reason I recognized him was that there had been a photograph of him with Anna that my grandmother had kept on her piano until her death.

"Where have you been?" Cynthia asked. "My God, we thought they'd taken you away. What was the problem?"

"Photographs on Rivers's computer. Have you found out if it's only our plane?"

"They haven't told us a thing. They just walk around and posture."

"There's a lot of posturing," Rivers agreed. "I suppose they feel threatened when this sort of thing happens. What is happening? Does anyone know?"

The tall good-looking redheaded man who had been *my aunt Anna's* editor and friend—if you want to remember how

wonderful and strange the world is even in the midst of disorder and the threat of disaster, which is probably the main
thing the human race has been in the midst of since we first
began as scared little lemurs, not to mention since we have
known how to make and use language and store knowledge
and talk about the future and the past—whose name was
Robert and whose photograph with Aunt Anna had been
on a piano *that I played* when I used to try to play, took over.
"It's a general threat to the airport and the city of London,"
McArthurs said. "We're going to be here for a while so put
some crackers in your pockets. They might run out of snacks
before too long." He laughed and smiled and looked at me.
"I'm Robert McArthurs. Which one of you is Miss Hand?"

"Me," I said stupidly. He really was an extraordinarily
handsome man. I held out my hand to him. "Louise Hand.
You were Anna's editor at Faber and Faber. I've read your
letters to her. It's lovely to meet you. What are you doing in
the airport? I thought you lived in London."

"I'm on my way to join my family in Turkey. They're on
holiday. If I'd had my radio on in the automobile I might have
known not to go into the airport. This started in London
several hours ago. They've closed the banks."

"So here we are," Rivers said. "Well, I'm going to try to
call my family. God knows what they're hearing on television." Everyone pulled out cellular phones and began trying
to make calls. Except me. I wasn't thinking about making

a cellular telephone call in the presence of a man as handsome as Robert McArthurs, even if he is happily married to a beautiful American journalist who nursed him back to health after a stroke he suffered in his thirties and about which he wrote a wonderful, lyrical, long article in *The New Yorker* that later became a book.

"I read your book about the stroke," I said. "I had already read the one you wrote about the English language. I have Anna's autographed copy."

"Tell me about your family," he said, settling into a seat beside me on the sofa and putting his elbows on his long legs and leaning toward me. "I stayed with your grandparents when I came to Charlotte, and then spent several days at your Uncle Daniel's house. Tell me where everyone is. Start with your grandparents."

"The family," I said, giggling. " 'These are the patterns that enthrall a genetic line. Power from the preceding generations hobbles the new generation.' I was thinking about that earlier today. I can't remember why."

" 'Are we doomed to repeat the patterns,' " he quoted. "She wrote that to me in a letter before she used it in the book. Where is the quotation from?"

"I don't know. About my family. Grandmother is still alive but very weak and bedridden. She is ninety-nine. Granddaddy died four years ago. All the Hands and Mannings live a long time. I guess I should have some long-term-care insurance but I don't. Anyway, the most interesting people are my cousin, Tallulah, who plays tennis, and my cousin, Scarlett, and my cousin, Daniel Davis, and who else, my sister, Laura, who is in medical school, and I guess you know about Uncle Daniel's daughter, Olivia. She's a writer. She wrote a history of the Cherokee Indian chief, Sequoyah, and now she's the editor of the Tulsa, Oklahoma, newspaper. She's the first woman editor. She keeps in touch with me. She wants to be a novelist but she can never get the novels published. She sends them to me to read. You'd like her if you met her. Everyone says she looks like Anna."

"Anna was so lovely. She shone with life. It is impossible that she died. And stupid. She could have been saved."

"We don't think so. No one in the family has ever been angry with her for doing it. She was a comet. She had to go that way. She couldn't be an invalid or a sick person. Everyone thinks that except for Grandmother. Grandmother thinks it was unholy and set a bad example."

"We're a strange generation, the one Anna and I belonged to. Your mother is the youngest, isn't she?"

"Louise, 'the most selfish girl on the planet,' as Anna described her in fiction without even changing her name. Momma thinks it's funny. She is selfish. She's had two face-lifts and she spends four weeks a year at a spa in Dallas. She looks younger than I do."

"What are you talking about?" Cynthia and Rivers and Mary Jane had finished their telephone conversations and were turned to us now.

"About my family," I said. "Robert came to my aunt's funeral in Charlotte and he came back later to look at manuscripts Aunt Helen found in Anna's papers. He knows everyone in the family. I was catching him up."

"They're exciting people," Mary Jane said. "Powerful and beautiful, all of them."

"Tell me about Daniel," Robert asked.

"He quit drinking. Uncle James, who is the oldest, got prostate cancer but has never treated it. He's had it for ten years and it hasn't gotten any worse. Then he got hunchbacked because he only has one lung from having polio when he was young so that scared Uncle Daniel and he quit drinking. He still acts just like he did though. He gardens and he's gone crazy for growing roses. And he takes care of Grandmother. He goes to see her every afternoon and they talk about all of us. I write her letters and he reads them to her."

"What is going on out there?" Cynthia said. She stood up. "Look out the window." We all got up and looked. The plane that was supposed to have been taking us to Italy was being backed away from the terminal. It was turning and taxiing toward a runway.

"There goes our chance of making it to the villa this weekend," Mary Jane said. "I don't suppose Cynthia's husband can get any of his money back, of course not."

"I'm going to the desk and see what's going on," I said.

"No, don't do that," Mary Jane said. "That won't do any good. It's our own fault. We should have known better than to leave home with everything that's going on in the world. So here we are."

"Bridge, anyone?" Robert suggested. "I can procure a deck of cards."

"Sure," Cynthia said, "I'll play. I used to play duplicate. I'm good."

"I will," Mary Jane said. "Who's a fourth?"

James Monroe, the man in tweeds, stood up and stretched his arms over his head. "I'll play," he said. "I'll take one of the ladies and you take the other one," he suggested to Robert. "That way if they overpower us at least they won't be a team."

"Robert McArthurs," Robert said and put out his hand.

"James Monroe," the man said and extended his own.

The British Airways agent came back to our table and told us they hoped to have flights out by four or five that afternoon. "We don't foresee you having to spend a night here," he added. "So please try to be patient. We're doing everything we can to end this crisis."

"The plane with our luggage just left the port," Cynthia said. "Tell me they are going to bring the luggage back."

"Where are they taking it?" Rivers began, but the agent had moved on to another group of stranded first-class passengers.

"His can't be a happy job," Robert offered.

"Flak catchers," Rivers said. "Having to deal with people like us who are accustomed to bossing people around. I get the feeling lately," she continued, "that most of my conversations are with people who work for me in one way or the other. I have two houses, and a lodge in Jackson Hole, Wyoming. I spend half my time talking to housekeepers, plumbers, roofers, painters, drapery hangers, window-blind installers, lawyers, or certified public accountants. I like them. I like people who work better than I like people like myself, which is why I do volunteer work. It's better than not working at all, which is the most boring thing in the world and why old people become morose. Still, I long for conversation with people who don't want anything from me. Like this. I feel fortunate to have run into all of you, even if it took a bomb scare to set it up."

"Then let's converse," Robert said. "I don't think anyone really wants to play bridge. Am I right?" The cards had been dealt but he was right, no one was really interested in playing cards.

"Let's choose a subject and expound on it," Rivers said. "Like the old Greeks used to do. There's plenty to talk about. Terrorism, religion, marriage, divorce, why young people are hard to control, if we should try to control them, if we should, for God's sake, have them."

"I'm in for that," I said. "I'm thirty-five years old and I haven't had a child and I'm worried that I haven't. I don't want to use old eggs. I want to have a child now but how can I? I don't live in a community. I leave on the spur of the moment to go anywhere. I don't love anyone enough to quit work and be a wife. And I sure don't want to be a single mother. That's so sad somehow. Nature tells me one thing. Watching my friends with their children tells me another, and besides, I have a mother that really isn't all that good at mothering me. She mostly concentrates on how I look. She thinks all will be well if you're beautiful or at least extremely well-groomed."

"She may be right," Rivers said. "Children are a mixed blessing, especially if you get some who don't like you, as I did. Besides my large-size daughter I have a son named Carl who blames everything on me. I'm his scapegoat. When I get a message from him on the message machine I heave sighs before I can stand to call him back. He married an Italian woman he met somewhere. She's mean to him and he blames me for that. I told him not to marry her but he wouldn't stop. Now it's been six years of hell for everyone. I have herpes simplex I picked up at church camp when I was a teenager. Nothing bad, just occasional fever blisters if I get upset. I hadn't had an outbreak in years until Carl married Maria. Every time I stay at their house I break out with fever blisters. Every time I visit them or they visit me. It's so indicative, I mean, evidence of things unseen. All that bad energy swarming around my child and grandchild, all that anger and Italian wine drinking and yelling. So am I glad I had Carl? I had him after three girls, and being the only boy in a houseful of sisters set him up to be bossed and yelled at. What else have my children done to pay me back for having them? The fat one, then the second one married a born-again Christian and goes to some dreadful, stupid church, and the third one lives at home and doesn't work."

"You have an eventful life," Robert said.

"My children are angels," Mary Jane said, "But I get tired of taking care of them all day. I feel guilty when I leave them. I'm feeling guilty now. I'll feel guilty the whole time I'm in Italy if we ever get there and when I get home they'll make me feel even guiltier and probably get sick while I'm gone to prove the point. They're six and seven. A boy and then a girl. They like to fight."

"My oldest child," Cynthia began, "The one who would eat chocolate pudding all day but I don't let her do it, also loves to watch television. She will do anything to get to watch the cartoon channel. I'm not sure she can read and she's in the second grade. She has no intellectual curiosity. I've always read and tried to think straight, and was a good student, wasn't I, Louise? I was going to nursing school at Vandy but then I met Darren and married him. I was glad to stop because organic chemistry was hard for me and I wasn't sure I was going to be able to continue so I might have married him as an excuse to quit. So I had Jane and she's not very bright. Darren's a lawyer, magna cum laude at Vandy. My father is a physician. There are lots of smart people in my family. Well, my mother is pretty dull but anyway, so I have this child who loves television. I love her but I don't feel guilty if I leave for two weeks. She'll get to watch television all the time while I'm gone and probably con the temporary nanny into letting her stay home from school half the days. She's good at pretending to be sick."

"I have two boys, ten and fourteen," Robert put in. "I've had a good time with them but it's becoming difficult. We caught the older boy with drugs last summer. At thirteen, God knows where he got them. We live in London. It's easy for anyone to get marijuana. And small towns aren't much better."

"People love to get high," I said. "I don't. I like to work. I'm ambitious. Maybe that's the same thing but I don't think so. We let our children see us drink. Then we let them drink, thinking they will learn how to drink intelligently, but most of them never do. They learn to use drugs and alcohol for props, for courage, for macho, for pain. They use amphetamines for study. In the high-octane lives we prepare them for there may not be a way to withstand the pain except getting high. You can't teach young people to meditate. It's unnatural. So we have this culture and we are killing ourselves and our children with it even when we aren't at war. What should we do about all that?"

"Stop a minute," James Monroe said. He stood up and spread open his hands. "You are thinking incorrectly. They are alive. If they are alive, your children are your blessings, your excitement, your entry to the future, both biologically and intellectually. I lost a grandson. If you only knew. I don't mean to preach but really, if they bother you, tell them so, and go on loving them. Don't let them make you feel guilty. That's up to you, I think. Anyone will press on someone who has power over them unless you move away. Don't let them press. If I had my grandson back he could weigh three hundred pounds and wear earrings. If I only knew he was still here, could see him, talk to him."

"Oh, God," I began. "Of course you're right. . . ."

There was a sudden blast, a sound, a terrible thunder that moved the floor. The window behind us buckled toward the runway and bellowed out. The shatterproof glass was holding for what seemed a long time, then it collapsed. Robert grabbed me and dragged me back into the center of the lounge. Everyone else ran and scrambled back around us as a second window collapsed.

"Where are the police?" Cynthia screamed. "Where are those soldiers? I thought they were all over the place. Was that luggage blowing up out there?"

"We don't know," I told her. "Sit down. Sit still. Take a breath. Take some deep breaths. We're in trouble here."

"Please proceed from the first-class lounge area into the concourse area," a voice over the loudspeaker was saying. "Please line up two abreast and leave the first-class lounge. There are doctors in the concourse if you are injured. Please hurry, but don't crowd one another."

We moved as a group toward the door. There were forty people in front of us being handed tags as they exited the lounge. "Please take all your belongings with you," the speaker announced. "Please proceed in a quiet manner toward the concourse. Do not crowd your fellow passengers. Please proceed in an orderly manner into the D concourse."

Rivers and I were together in line, then Cynthia and Mary Jane, then Robert McArthurs and James Monroe, then the Chinese mother and daughter. We passed through the doors into the concourse and were given a second set of tags to wear around our necks and then herded toward tables where people with notebooks were writing down names.

The concourse was quiet except for some piped-in music, which no one had remembered to turn off. Johann Sebastian Bach's Toccata and Fugue in D Minor was playing. I looked back at Robert and pointed into the air and he smiled and held out his hand as though to play the bass clef on a keyboard.

"What?" Cynthia demanded. "What are you doing?"

"The sound of Western civilization," I answered, loving her very much for being herself and no one else. "It's a piece I love by Bach. In my failed novel I had Elise play it for herself before she walked out the door to go drive her automobile into the frozen lake, when I was trying to make sense of Aunt Anna's suicide. The book was a complete failure but I learned a lot from writing it."

"What did you learn?" Rivers asked.

"That I am not a fiction writer, certainly not a novelist, and, more important, that suicide really is a mistake and not fair to the ones who are left behind."

"I disagree," Mary Jane said. "If you are in great pain or about to be, you get to end your life. I sure haven't been in charge of myself all these years to leave my death in the hands of fate."

"Me either," James Monroe put in. "Well put."

The Toccata and Fugue in D Minor was interrupted by an announcement. "There has been an explosion in a petrol supply truck. There are no casualties. This was not, we repeat, not caused by a bomb but by human error. There is no cause for alarm. Stay calm. We expect to have the airport running again by evening. If you need help there are stations in every concourse."

"I say." James Monroe had taken Robert's arm. "I wonder if they could supply me with portable oxygen. Heart problem, probably not life-threatening. I'm a director of Lloyd's. We insure these airplanes, actually." He had begun to breathe with difficulty and both Mary Jane and Robert began moving with him to the front of the line. The line didn't seem to be accomplishing much except giving everyone a place to be, but when I got to the head of it they checked my airline ticket, offered help if needed, and when I told them I worked for PBS and BBC and showed them my press credentials, they opened up and gave me all the information they had. It wasn't much. There had been bombings in downtown London and threats to Heathrow, but the explosion had indeed—"indeed," they kept repeating—been caused by carelessness and had nothing, repeat nothing, to do with terrorism.

"As if I'm going to believe that any more than I believe all those wildfires in southern California are caused by campfires," Cynthia said to me in a quiet voice. Once again I loved her so much for being herself that I could barely stand it.

"How have we lost each other all these years," I said. "Your 'little voice,' you used to use that when we'd whisper in class. Remember in Mrs. Jarvis's room at Southern Seminary and you'd tell me all the gossip when she was writing on the blackboard?"

"She liked to write on the blackboard more than anyone I have ever known in my life," Cynthia answered. "She would write down whole poems with all the punctuation, then read them to us, then make us read them."

"Or make us copy them and she was supposed to be teaching history."

"She was a doll. Let's write her a postcard and tell her where we are. How could we find out her address?"

"We'll send it to the school, to the History Department. Surely by now she has a medal of honor or a portrait in Hancock Hall. I saw something about her in an alumni newsletter not long ago. I bet she's still alive."

"Let's buy postcards and write to everyone we can think of."

"Great idea." I turned around and told Cynthia's idea to Rivers and she wanted in, so as soon as we finished in the line we found a shop that was miraculously still open and began to pick out cards.

The second explosion shook the building's floor and foundation. Things in the shop fell from their shelves and we huddled together in the middle of the magazine section. Rivers grabbed me by the sleeve and began to pull me out of the shop. "Get to clear ground," she said. "I know earthquakes. I'm telling you, get out of here." She yelled at the shop girl to follow us and we moved out into the area where the lines had formed to show tickets. We each had a handful of postcards. When we settled down on the floor in a cleared place, Rivers handed the shop girl a twenty-dollar bill but the girl wouldn't take it. She was crying and I began to try to calm her.

"Human error, we repeat, human error," Cynthia said. "You bet it's human error. Error to leave home during a worldwide crisis. Error to think we can run free and democratic societies with this madness all around us. Oh, God, I have to talk to my children. What are we doing here? Call someone, Louise. Get us out of here."

"The ventilation systems are unharmed." A voice came through the speakers. "We have the airport under control. *The airport is under control.* Stay calm, stay where you are. Do not panic." The voice repeated that message several times, then added, "The initial explosion was caused by human error near a petrol truck. The second explosion was indeed an explosive device, but we have found the others and all will be well. There will not be further explosions. Stay where you are. Remain calm. Do not panic or attempt to leave your area." This second message was repeated several times, then the Toccata and Fugue in D Minor came back on and I sat back, patting the shop girl's arm and listening to the music and I began to think I really was, after all, helpless. After all the bravado of my thirty-five years, after all the opinions and education and help from people like Mrs. Harriet Jarvis and all the travel and work and friends and books and paintings and beautiful clothes and hotels and automobiles I was just as helpless as the smallest insect crawling across my white tile bathroom floor that I stepped on with my house slipper, always being remorseful when I killed it and always remembering Salinger and Seymour Glass teaching me Zen Buddhism, which I may or may not have understood or learned.

The heavenly music written by the genius Johann Sebastian Bach kept on playing and I kept on patting the arm of the sweet, brown-haired shop girl and Rivers and Cynthia sat beside me doing breathing exercises, as the concourse filled with soldiers.

After what seemed a short while but was probably almost an hour we all started to feel better about things and the shop girl went back to the shop and picked up some bags of chips and a few health snack bars and brought them to us and we found folding chairs and sat on them and began to write postcards. We alternated between writing post-cards and trying to make cellular telephone calls to people who were worried about us. Robert McArthurs and Charles Halliday returned to our group but James Monroe, who had turned out to be the chairman of the world-famous insur-ance company that insures the queen's jewels and the air-planes of British Airways, had been whisked off to receive further medical treatment.

"So does all this change anyone's mind about whether it's a good idea to have children in 2004?" Rivers asked. "I'd like to go back to that if no one minds?"

"What would be the alternative?" Robert asked. "Just let the human race die out? Except only Western civiliza-tion would die out, our upper-middle-class part of it, since Africa and India have proven that people will continue to reproduce under the worst imaginable circumstances, not to mention the circumstances in which the first twenty-five million years of human evolution proceeded."

"But the question is," Mary Jane said, "whether edu-cated people knowing what we know would go on having children."

"They might not until the birth control pills ran out," Cynthia said. "Then they'd go back to having babies the way we used to have them all those twenty-five million years, which is girls having them the first year they ovulate and the babies are probably stronger and the grandmothers take care of them and life would insist on itself. It wouldn't die out. It wouldn't let itself die out. I'm going home, everyone. As soon as this calms down I'm going back to my house and my children."

"Don't do that," I said. "Give us a few days with you in the villa your husband paid for. Don't throw away his gift to you."

"I'll come by and see you," Robert said. "I have an author in Florence I need to visit. Perhaps I can wangle an airline ticket out of the paper and come have an evening while we're all on holiday."

WESTERN CIVILIZATION WON its battles on this nineteenth day of April, 2004. By six that afternoon Heathrow Airport was secured by British forces. By seven that evening airplanes were taking off for their destinations. Fifteen people had been arrested in London and every inch of Heathrow had been searched. Two more explosive devices had been found and defused but the authorities still insisted the first explosion had been caused by human error. Rumor had it that it had been a cigarette thrown on the ground by a tired dog handler and that he had confessed and asked to be forgiven.

. . .

AT ELEVEN THAT night Mary Jane, Cynthia, Rivers, and I boarded a British Airways jet bound for Pisa, Italy. We had convinced Rivers to come with us to the villa to decompress before she pressed on to Florence. "We have cars with drivers at the villa," Cynthia told her. "You shouldn't go to a major city until all this calms down. We'll want to go into Florence in a few days so we'll take you."

"I will go with you then," Rivers said. "I don't feel like traveling alone after all of this."

Robert McArthurs left on a flight at ten. Charles Halliday left at ten fifteen, after giving us his cards, writing down our addresses, and promising to keep in touch. "Christmas cards and notices," he promised. "My list is getting short, due to the grim reaper. I need fresh ladies to dream about."

"We'll answer," Mary Jane assured him. "I don't think any of us is going to forget this day or the people who were with us."

By then we had all managed to talk to people at home or at least get messages delivered. "Tell them it was nothing," Rivers kept saying. "Or they'll come and get us like in *The Ambassadors* by Henry James."

"Go to Arezzo and see the 'Legend of the True Cross' by Piero della Francesca," Robert McArthurs said as he was leaving. He dropped his bags and scribbled a name and number on a piece of paper and handed it to me. "Believe me,

Louise, in the name of all that's holy and in memory of your Aunt Anna, don't forget to do this. It isn't far from Vorno and this man will be your guide and see that you get tickets if you can't get them any other way."

"What is it?" I asked. "Why do you need tickets?"

"It's a very holy sight," he said. "It is art at its most real and useful and divine. Trust me. Trust your Aunt Anna. You need tickets," he added, pulling his bag back onto his shoulder, "because it is a very small chapel on a quiet street and they still let people go in and look at the mural, but they only let in about ten at a time and only so many on any day. There's a coffee shop across the street where Anna and I had coffee and croissants when we were there. It was raining and we giggled with delight both before and after we saw the paintings. Remember me. Send me a postcard."

"Where should I send it?" I called after him.

"To the *London Telegraph*. You can find the number." Then he was gone, the legendary Robert McArthurs, who had been so much a part of Anna's life when she first was famous and whose beautiful letters to her I had read when I was a teenager and used to like to go through the boxes of Anna's things Aunt Helen had stored in grandmother's attic. The papers went to universities, some to Duke and some to Chapel Hill. "We should have kept those papers for a while," I grumbled.

Rivers and Mary Jane came up to me. "Are you all right?" Rivers asked.

"I hate for Robert to leave. I hate for this to end. It's been an adventure, hasn't it?"

"We'll have a better one when we get to the villa," Cynthia promised, joining us. "Come on, let's stay together. They might call our flight at any time."

We arrived at the Leonardo da Vinci airport in Pisa with the sky still full of stars and were met by an Englishman named Paul who runs the villa, and by a beautiful, bilingual woman named Claudia who had left a famous Italian tennis player to come back to Vorno and be second in command at the fourteenth-century villa that cost twenty-six thousand dollars a week to rent. "Movie stars usually rent this place," Cynthia had explained when I went aghast at the cost. "They're glad to have some normal people. Darren got a cut rate, but he always says that whether he actually does or not."

The villa was outside the small town of Vorno, which is seven miles from the ancient walled city of Lucca. We were driven there in two Mercedes with a van following with the luggage. It was still dark when we drove through Vorno and out to the villa but by the time we arrived daylight was beginning to light up the hills and the roses on the stone walls and the sculpture on the façades and the steeples of the stone chapel. Two maids in black dresses with white lace aprons served us coffee in the front patio and then we wandered inside to choose our rooms. Cynthia had been assigned the master suite with a ten-foot-square hot tub but she kept trying to give it to one of us.

There were eight compartments. Most of us chose ones in the back on the top floor, but Rivers took a smaller bed and bath on the front of the house near the entrance hall. Some of our luggage had not arrived and she said she wanted to be near the door to hear her suitcase come in.

OUR FIRST NIGHT at the villa we had a meeting with Paul and Claudia before dinner. We met in the beautiful garden behind the house. There was a fountain and a pool and lemon trees all overlooking and sloping down toward a grass tennis court. We had white wine and cheese and Paul asked us where we would like to go on Thursday and Friday, which were the only weekdays left of the week.

"To Arezzo," I said. "Wherever that is."

"And to see the coast," Cynthia said. "Even if it's still too cold to swim I'd like to see it."

"The Italian Riviera?" Mary Jane asked. "That's near here?"

"Not exactly," Paul answered. "At least we don't call it that. It's the Versilian Coast, Forte dei Marmi and Viareggio."

"Let's go there on Thursday and to Arezzo on Friday then," Cynthia said.

"Whatever you want. There are cars with drivers but Claudia and I could take you if you'd rather have us do it. It isn't far."

"We'll use the drivers," Cynthia decided. "Since they are paid for anyway."

WE HAD A lovely dinner, salad and pasta and broiled fish with a divine sauce and then a chocolate pastry filled with hot liquid chocolate and covered with ice cream or whipped cream or both. Then coffee on the terrace, no bugs, then off to bed. I took an Ambien so I would get on native time and so did Cynthia. Mary Jane is afraid to take pills since she was almost an alcoholic at one time. Rivers said she always just gutted it out about jet lags.

TWO DAYS LATER we made our pilgrimage to Arezzo. Rivers had decided to stay and go with us. "I'm not crazy enough not to enjoy life after what we just witnessed in London," she declared. "Who knows, maybe I'll be the one to introduce Piero della Francesca to Jackson, Mississippi."

"You can't move a mural," Cynthia said. "I don't think you can."

"Yes, but you can film it and show the film."

Claudia had made reservations for us at the church in

Arezzo, the kitchen had packed lunches, and the twin Mercedes were waiting with their drivers.

We had breakfast at seven, then got into the cars and started moving. Our first reservation was at nine. The second group was going in at nine forty-five. "You can stay in the church longer if you like," Claudia said. "They never make people leave since only ten go in at a time. It's very quiet and beautiful. You have the place to yourself. The little town is beautiful. When you finish you'll want to wander around, then if you like you can have a picnic at the ruins of a palazzo. We called ahead, they'll be expecting you there. I'd take my cameras if I were you, but, of course, you can't take them into the church."

Cynthia took a camera, but then, no one is perfect. She and I drew the first tickets and left Mary Jane and Rivers to drink coffee in the café where Aunt Anna and Robert McArthurs had drunk coffee in the rain so many years ago. The café looked as though it had not changed in fifty years, much less twenty.

"If I get a chance to take a photograph I'm going to," Cynthia whispered to me, as we approached the church.

"I'll buy you a poster if you don't," I answered. "I love you, Cyn, but you have to respect their rules." I hugged her to make up for not being a good conspirator. "Think of the headlines. *Tri-Delts caught sneaking photographs in Arezzo*. It might affect rush."

"Oh, shut up," she said. "You've changed, Louise. You really have."

"I'll be thirty-six years old in January," I answered. "I hope to God I've changed." Then an old priest opened the doors to the Chiesa di San Francesco, a church so old and beautiful that it seemed it must have been built by angels and certainly guarded by them, and we entered. Even if I hadn't told her not to I don't think Cynthia or anyone would have used a flash camera in the still, dark mystery of the stone church painted with the beautiful murals of Piero della Francesca. The murals tell the story of the finding of the true cross by people wearing robes of such lush colors it is impossible to believe the paint could be six hundred years old. Angels indeed. Angels for sure.

We stayed a long, long time and then held hands and walked out and went across the street and told Mary Jane and Rivers it was their turn to go inside.

Now it was mine and Cynthia's turn to sit in the café looking across the bricked street to the church and hold hands and drink coffee and eat croissants and write postcards to Robert McArthurs thanking him for telling us about this treasure.

"Thank you for bringing me here," I said to my old friend and sister in Tri-Delt. "I'm sorry I got huffy about the camera."

"You were right," she said. "I'll never forget this day. It makes up for Heathrow, doesn't it?"

"Life on the Planet Earth," I answered. "Wars and strife and surprises and love and children and art. I've made up my mind about children, by the way. I'm going out and get set to have some. This is our parade and I'm marching in it." She squeezed my hand and we went back to writing on our postcards and eating croissants and being here, glad to be alive in the only world there is, alive and eating and still breathing and not afraid really of anything that might happen next. We were Americans, for God's sake, we weren't in the habit of being afraid.

The Dogs

Dear New Neighbors,

I was out in my yard this afternoon and noticed the man you hired to repair the fence between our property. It's my fence by the way, but I'm glad to share it. Let me introduce myself. My name is Rhoda Manning and I live behind you in the Carl Jeans house. I also own the lot beside us to the north.

The fence man said you have three dogs. I hope they don't bark as I live very quietly. I am a writer and work

in my house so it is important for me to have quiet in
the mornings. Or while I'm sleeping in the afternoons. I
bought the empty lot to keep anyone from starting a building project while I am working.

I was bitten by a dog several years ago and am very sen-
sitive to dogs barking. I know you won't let them become a
problem and I welcome you to our neighborhood and hope
to meet you soon. If you see me in the backyard please call
and come over.

There used to be a stile between our yards but the past
owner of your house asked me to take it down as he had a
nice, quiet sheepdog who liked to escape by climbing it.

I miss the stile. I used to climb it pulling hoses to water
the trees on the lot. I hope you enjoy the trees, especially
this fall when they turn glorious colors. There are six sugar
maples, three oaks, and one lonely little dogwood that
isn't doing very well. The daughter of our neighbors on
the other side, Jenny and Bob Hingis, used to water the
trees for me when she and they were young. She is a gifted
pianist who is at the University of Chicago now studying
music. Anyway, welcome to Lighton Trail.

With all good wishes,
Rhoda Manning

September 29, 2002

Dear Neighbors,

I hate to complain but your dogs have been barking all afternoon for several weeks now and I can't get any work done and can't sleep. I get up early to work and need to sleep in the afternoon as I am not young. I am sixty-seven.

I'm sure you will fix this problem. I'm really sorry we haven't met. I came by to meet you but you weren't there so I went home and wrote this letter. My phone number is 443-5566. Please call or come over and we can talk. Also, forgive that pile of lumber on the lot. The past owner of your house threw it over there and promised to move it, but he never did. I'm sure he just forgot. Anyway, please put the dogs up in the afternoon while I'm trying to sleep.

All good wishes,
Rhoda Manning

Jennings, Harding, Young, Catesby and Foster
Attorneys at Law
13 Centre Street
Michlen, Mississippi

Dear Ms. Manning,

Thank you for your letter welcoming us to the neighborhood. We are sorry our dogs are disturbing you but this is a neighborhood and dogs bark and noise is made. We are making every effort to keep our dogs quiet but we can't be expected to live our lives so that you can take two-hour naps in the afternoon.

As to the mess on the lot I am not responsible for verbal agreements you made with Mr. Horn.

I love my animals and will keep your letters in case anything unusual happens to them. I would take it very seriously if any harm came to them.

Sincerely,
Layton Morris Foster

October 3, 2002
To Thomas Little, Attorney at Law
Jackson Mississippi

Dear Thomas,

I am enclosing this threatening letter I got from my new neighbor. I wrote him two nice, kind letters welcoming him to the neighborhood and asking him not to let his dogs bark. I didn't hear anything after the first one and after the second one I got this. It's true I don't like dogs much, especially since the Deneves' dog practically destroyed my right leg. You got me ten thousand dollars for that, if you remember. I should have taken your advice and held out for more as I have a terrible scar as you predicted I would. Plus, my fear of strange dogs. Anyway, imagine the nerve of this guy saying he will save my letters. Not to mention writing to me on law firm stationery. I wish I could tell him my cousin is the Chief Justice of the Fifth Circuit Court of Appeals but I'm too well raised to tell him. Maybe you should tell him.

Will you write him a letter? If that doesn't work we can tell one of his senior partners what he's doing to me. I work out at the gym with Bob Harding and used to fuck Terry Jennings.

I love you. Stay well and let's have lunch soon. I miss you.

Rhoda

Dear Rhoda,

I'll talk to the city attorney about it first. Then we can go to Bob Harding and ask him to jerk Mr. Foster's string. He's probably some hot-shot kid just out of law school. Sorry about the dogs keeping you from sleeping. That's always so annoying. Anna and I have been wondering why you don't come to Jackson. Where have you been? We need to talk about the new episodes of *The Sopranos*.

All best,

Thomas

Later —

I talked to the city attorney and he said this Foster kid was handling a matter for them so it's tricky for him to get involved but he'll say something to him when they meet next week to talk about the city's case. Someone's suing the city jail.

Be of good cheer. I'll always take care of you.

I think the third episode was pure genius but can't get anyone around here to agree with me. Anna won't watch it, says it's too violent. Let me hear from you.

Love,
Thomas

I have a trial coming up on the coast. I'll get in touch when I come back. It's Murder One. I'm too old for this.

November 5, 2002

Memo: From Rhoda Katherine Manning to all my neighbors

Help! I know I am not the only one who is being driven crazy by the pack of dogs Layton Foster has put in his back-yard. They bark all night and they bark all day. If I go out in my backyard they charge the fence (my fence) and act like they are going to tear me to pieces. I am sleepless. I am enraged and the city dog-control people are not being very helpful. Please get back to me if you share this problem.

November 6, 2002

Dear Mr. and Mrs. Foster,

We, along with Rhoda Manning and Olivia and William Carter, being greatly distressed due to the behavior of your dogs, are sending you this formal complaint.

Ever since you moved into your house this problem has been growing. The dogs bark continuously while you are gone. If any of us go out into our backyards they throw themselves against our fences and bark and threaten us. I am afraid to let my grandchildren in the backyard for fear the black one will bite them through my flimsy fence. When we try to work in our garden or trim our hedges they bark continuously. If we even open our screen doors they rush to the fence and bark and threaten us. Also they are trying to dig through the fence.

All of us have also heard them barking at night. We have all made complaints to city officials and we know they have called you to register our complaints but you have done nothing to stop the behavior of your dogs. We hope you and your wife will meet with us about this problem. Otherwise we will all five take the matter to the City Prosecutor and proceed accordingly.

Please call and let us know if you want to meet with us. Our phone number is 998-7766.

Yours Truly,

Jenny and Bob Hingis

Copies to:

Rhoda Manning

Olivia and William Carter

Harvey Colten, M.D. (Behind Lighton Trail on Corner of
Amethyst Hill and Rockcrest)

Dear Dr. and Mrs. Foster,

My husband and I are joining Rhoda Manning and Jenny
and Bob Hingis in their complaint against your animals.
We are animal lovers ourselves and have an aging dog and
two gravely ill cats. Wes spend most of our reserve cash
at the veterinarian's trying to keep those cats alive. So you
can see this is not about your having animals in general.
It is about the constant barking that has caused us to stay
inside during the lovely fall weather. We spent sixty thousand dollars to have a porch built on the back of our house
so we could enjoy our yard in the nice weather. Now,
when we go out on the porch, all we see are dogs barking
and threatening us at our fence. This is especially disturbing when we have company. Children won't go in our yard
because the black dog throws himself against the fence.

Yours sincerely,

William and Olivia Carter

Copies to:

Rhoda Manning

Jenny and Bob Hingis

Harvey Colton, M.D. (house on corner)

Thomas Little, Attorney at Law

November 18, 2002

Dear Rhoda Manning, Jenny and Bob Hingis, William and
Olivia Carter, Harvey Colton, M.D.,

When I bought this house I was told by the Harrisons
that this was a friendly neighborhood. So far none of you
have stopped by to tell us hello or introduce yourselves.
I have had these dogs for many years. They are not a nui-
sance and no one has ever complained about them before.
They only bark when they are excited. There have been
a lot of workmen in our backyard since we bought the
house. Also, the cable people were digging both in my
yard and on Ms. Manning's lot and that has disturbed
them. What do you all want me to do? I cannot leave the
poor creatures inside all day. Nor, as Miss Manning suggested, do we want to build new fences in our yard, cutting our yard in two for all practical purposes, in order
to keep them away from your fences. Please stop leaving
ugly letters in my mailbox or this is going to stop being a

neighborhood affair. As I told Ms. Manning, I am saving all the letters. If anything untoward ever happens to my dogs I will have them.

> Yours sincerely,
> Layton Foster

November 20, 2002

Dear Mr. and Mrs. Foster,

Please be advised that on Saturday I am having my back fence removed. It is old and flimsy and I am planning on replacing it with dogwood trees and azalea bushes along the fence row in the spring.

> Yours sincerely,
> Rhoda Manning

Copies to Bob and Jenny Hingis, Olivia and William Carter, Thomas Little, Attorney at Law, Harvey Colton, M.D.

Dear Rhoda,

We are elated that you are taking down your fence! ! ! ! ! ! ! I don't think we are getting anywhere with the Fosters. They are lying about everything. I went over to talk to their old neighbors and people on both sides said their dogs barked night and day (incessantly) when they lived there and they did nothing to stop it, even when they were in the yard with them.

Bob and I are afraid they will poison or shoot one of the dogs and try to blame it on us. He has already threatened both you and us with that possibility. Are you sure your lawyer in Jackson is staying on top of this? Bob thinks we should take all the correspondences to our lawyer also and file some sort of suit.

Our worry is that the dogs will get sick and he'll say we poisoned them. Even the allegation would be damaging to any of us, as we all have positions in the community. My cousin, Arthur Williams, is an attorney and would take care of this if you aren't sure your attorney in Jackson is doing it. Give us a call.

Thanks for your time,
Jenny Hingis
Bob Hingis

Copies to:
Harvey Colton, M.D.
Olivia and William Carter
Arthur Williams, Atty. At Law
Thomas Little, Atty. At Law

November 22, 2002

Dear Squabbling Neighbors,

I live in the yellow three-story house with the metal roof across the street from Rhoda Manning's lot and cater-cornered (sp?) from the alleged threatening and barking dogs. Yes, they bark. But mostly in the daytime and that's a blessing.

The Fosters have been putting copies of all your correspondence in my mailbox and although I had decided to recuse myself from your fun and games I have decided to take this opportunity to write to all of you about the cruelty and stupidity of keeping dogs for pets in the city to begin with.

Dogs are herd animals. They mark territory and defend it, mate when they smell a female in heat, follow alpha males to search for food, defecate to leave messages, carry ticks, fleas, and parasites from one place to another (they are the servants of their parasites, as we are also, but that's another matter). They are also funny and friendly and love to run and bark and show off and fight, all perfectly understandable mammalian behavior.

In order to turn them into PETS (disgusting word) and use them for surrogate children, love objects, or followers (this is very important especially to people who can't engender respect and love in their peers), modern man has decided to overfeed them, tie them up, pen them up, bore them to death, neuter them, drag them around on leashes for "walks," and in other words treat them like prisoners.

If they bark we throw water on them, put collars on them that give them electric shocks, squirt unpleasant odors into their nostrils, or tie them up in dark garages.

If you need to keep animals for friends and surrogate children you should move out to the country where they can run free and mate and have lives. IF you insist on keeping them in the city you must clean up their feces and keep them quiet. You are all dogs as far as I am concerned and so far away from any real humanity it is laughable to read your letters and your pitiful attempts to appear rational.

From my reading of your letters it looks to me like all of you keep dogs for prisoners except Ms. Manning, and she says the only reason she stopped is that one bit her.

My advice to all of you is to take all the dogs out into the country and turn them loose so they will have at least a few days of freedom in their lives. Then come back to town, put on sackcloth and ashes, and sign up to teach children to read and do math.

> Harvey Colton, M.D.,
> Author of *We Come from
> Risen Apes, Not Fallen Angels*
> Harvard University Press,
> 1986

Copies to:

R. Manning

B and J Hingis

Fosters

Carters

Little and Bordeaux, Attorneys at Law

14 Lafayette Street

Jackson, Mississippi

November 27, 2002

Dear Rhoda,

I think this needs to be settled before you end up in a law suit and I have to handle it. Please try to get everyone together at your house next weekend and I'll come and join you. I can't do it any sooner because I have to be on the coast until then.

I know the dogs are keeping you awake but please hold on until I return and don't write any more letters to your neighbors.

Be of good cheer. I think it was a little over the top for Tony to beat up the man who was screwing his little Russian mistress but Shakespeare wouldn't have stopped there. He would have had him kill him. I wish the show lasted three hours every Sunday night.

> Be of good cheer. I'll take
> care of you. With love,
> Thomas

Dear Neighbors,

Please all come to my house on Saturday afternoon, the
28th of November. My lawyer from Jackson will be here to
advise us. We have to get this settled. Layton, I have told the
workmen not to take down my fence until we have a meeting so please join the rest of us on Saturday, November 28.

>Peacefully yours,
>
>Rhoda Manning

Dear Thomas,

There is a god. The dogs are gone, disappeared. We
heard they took them to their old house on Maple Street
and shut them up in the yard over there. No one's living
in the house. They're trying to sell it. I feel sorry for the
neighbors over there but they're mostly a bunch of old field
hippies and if they cared they could do something about it
like we have been doing.

Thanks so much for your help. Good luck with the trial
on the coast. I've been reading about it in the paper. I don't
know what kind of outcome you are hoping for.

The new episodes of *The Sopranos* are brilliant but it's
being written by too many people. They are going to lay
down all these plot lines and then disappear for another
year. I wish I wasn't hooked on it. If Tony would fuck Dr.
Melfi I'd quit watching. Or if he found out about her rape
and killed her rapist. I wish I could write it.

>Meanwhile, onward,
>
>Rhoda

December 10, 2002

Dear Neighbors,

I am having my publisher send you each a hardback copy
of my book, *We Come from Risen Apes, Not Fallen Angels.* I
hope you take the time to read it.

I am negotiating with the city to take in some children
from Tin Cup for after-school instruction and play. Since
the little Hingis girl has gone to college there is no one to
sell me magazines, cookies, or Christmas wrapping paper.
A childless neighborhood is too dreary an affair for an old
romantic like myself.

I notice that the dogs are no longer in the Fosters's yard
so I assume you have come to some conclusion about all
of that.

Happy Holidays to all of you. I hope you enjoy the book.

Yours truly,

Harvey Colton, M.D.

December 11, 2002

Dear Rhoda,

I don't know what we have done here. The Fosters have
put their house up for sale and have bought a place out in
Madison County.

Dr. Colton has applied to the city for a permit to let
someone operate a day-care center for abused children in

his house. The fence people have already been over there measuring the yard. One of those elegant four-thousand-dollar swing sets is already installed and they are digging a hole for what is either a swimming pool or a ground-level trampoline. Do you think he would really do that?

We have been trying to read the book he sent to us but I think it is an atheist (sp?) tract. I mean, I don't have anything against atheists or abused children but why in our neighborhood? Is there anything we can do about this?

Your neighbors,
Olivia and William Carter

December 13, 2002

Dear Olivia and William,

I'm sorry. I know it's not across the street from me but even if it was I would not care if Dr. Colton starts a day-care center. Children are pretty, they don't carry fleas, and they *don't bark.* I like the book. I think it's brilliant, if slightly overwritten.

Actually, I can't think of a better outcome from all this than to have the Fosters move out to the country with their dogs. Merry Christmas to all of you. I'm going to the coast for a while. I don't want to get too insular if I can help it.

Yours in the neighborhood,
Rhoda

Dear Olivia and William,

I think I should warn you that Rhoda Manning is now seeing (maybe sleeping with) Dr. Colton. Bob and I ran into them out at the Walmart Supercenter where they had a cart full of Lego sets and Barbie dolls. They had an Irish Barbie, an Asian Barbie, and two Rapunzel Barbies, one Afro-American, one White.

Plus, his BMW was parked in her driveway all night on Saturday night. I thought she had left town to go to the coast!

If you are as concerned as we are about the pending day-care center please call tonight and let's talk. There is just no point in starting that on Lighton Trail, is there?

It's always something, isn't it?

> Yours sincerely,
> Bob Hingis
> Jenny Hingis

December 21, 2002

Dear Thomas,

I wrote the producers and told them either Dr. Melfi and Tony fuck each other or I'm canceling HBO. It won't be on again for ten months so what are we going to do now?

I may drive up to Jackson next week and take you to lunch and let you meet a new friend of mine. I am enclosing a copy of his book, We Come from Risen Apes, Not Fallen Angels. It's overwritten but the theory is sound. Didn't Tony look like a perfect ape in the episode where he was standing over the guy who was fucking the Russian girl. He had his belt doubled up in his hand just like the apes wield sticks they pick up from the forest floor.

Meanwhile, onward,
Rhoda

Postscript: No, I am not getting laid but I am thinking about it. Just one more time and then I'll quit for good. Maybe I won't do it. Maybe I'll go skiing instead. Sometimes I wish I would get cancer. Here would be my chemotherapy. Go skiing at Aspen on West Buttermilk. Charter a plane and fly somewhere to watch André Agassi play tennis. Fuck one of my old boyfriends, the one in New Orleans who got away would be nice or maybe the running back. Or just talk to them.

What else? Buy all my children and grandchildren who can drive new cars.

Buy Annie and Juliet one of those Barbie cars to drive around the yard.

Let you know how much you mean to me.

Happy Winter Solstice,

Love,
Rhoda

The Dissolution
of the Myelin Sheath

Multiple sclerosis is tricky," Dr. Anderson said, on a beautiful late summer day in Biloxi, with no storms brewing in the Gulf of Mexico and none expected. "Just because it seems to be getting worse doesn't mean it's a steady decline. So many things play into the progression. I want to try a new regimen they're having success with in Cincinnati. I was there last month for a seminar and I think it's worth trying. It could help you walk longer."

"Or not?" she answered. She was still beautiful and still charming and she used it. "I think I'll wait awhile before

I change medications. Is this bad news, Will, or just what you've been expecting?"

He didn't answer right away. "It's not good news."

"Because there isn't going to be any good news, right?"

"I'd like to try this new regimen. You've handled this so well, Philipa." He handed her a prescription. "Your sleeping pills. Is there anything else you need?"

"No, just the truth and you always give me that. I know it's hard to treat the untreatable."

"In Cincinnati I got excited at some of the results. The drugs may make you queasy at first, but I'd like to try them."

"I'd better go. You have an office full of patients. My insurance doesn't pay you enough. I wish you'd let us pay you extra money. Charles told me to tell you that."

"I'm fine. I'd like to see you again in two weeks. I'm proud of how you've handled this, Philipa."

"Oh, well, what were the options?" She smiled and gathered up her things and went out and down a long hall to a checkout desk and turned in her paperwork.

"He wants to see you again in two weeks. And he wants you to get blood work at the hospital." The nurse handed her more paper.

"I'll call," Philipa said. "I'll call next week." She turned some of the charm on the overweight woman with the pretty face who had been checking her in and out for what seemed like forever. "I'll call soon."

SHE WENT OUT to the parking lot and got into the new Mercedes with the special hand-operated foot pedals and the six huge airbags that sooner or later would probably go off and asphyxiate her. I finally got to use that word, she thought as she always did when she noticed the airbags. *Asphyxiate.* Keller and I used to know every word in the dictionary. We used to learn a word a day when we were young.

She laughed out loud thinking about her happy, happy childhood and her little brother, Keller, in his cowboy boots. All gone now, she remembered. Momma and Daddy and my aunts and uncles and grandparents and Keller having heart surgery and taking drugs that make him dumb, just to keep it beating. I thought we were so strong that we could never die.

She pulled down the rearview mirror and opened it and looked at herself while she slapped her cheeks with her left hand. Shut up. You have four children and countless grandchildren and a great-grandchild. You have lived a blessed life except for the dissolution of the fucking myelin sheath. You have tons of money and a great husband and a wonderful masseuse and friends if you'd ever call them up. You have good doctors who pay attention. You've had a wonderful life and now you need to find a way to asphyxiate yourself. Done deal. No turning back this time.

She was strangely happy. Having a plan always did that for her. She stopped at a drugstore and filled the prescription the doctor had given her.

THE MAIN THING is not to talk to anyone about anything that's wrong with me. Not the children, not Charles. Lie to him, lie to him, lie to him. So he won't feel like an accomplice. So he won't think he could have stopped it. Let him be mad at me. It will help him get over it. He's still a handsome man. Someone will marry him. Someone will always take care of a handsome man. What a relief it may be to him, after this mess I've put him through.

WHEN SHE GOT home Charles was waiting for her. "What did he tell you?" he asked. "What did he say?"

"That it's progressing and he wants to start me on some new regimen he learned in Cincinnati last week."

"You need to go to Duke or Mayo's. You need to go where the cutting-edge work is being done."

"He thinks it's being done in Cincinnati."

"I don't know. How do you feel?"

"Just like I did this morning and yesterday. It's progressing.

But I'm still walking. So let's don't talk about it. Let's call Salvetti's and have them deliver Italian food. I'm hungry for Italian food."

"I'm not happy with what you're doing with Anderson. I want you at a great hospital."

"I'm fine, Charles. Call Salvetti's and order something good to eat. I'm going to change clothes." She left him in the living room and went into her bedroom and took off her dress and put on a pair of slacks and a linen blouse.

An hour later they were in the dining room eating lasagna and fresh bread and drinking wine. "Don't worry about me," she was saying. "We're seventy-eight years old, Charles. What did we think was going to happen? At least you're in good health. At least we aren't both invalids. Actually, I like this disease. The dissolution of the myelin sheath, probably caused by a defect in the genes. It has a nice ring, doesn't it?

"And yes, right now it's bad news but not terrible news. And Doctor Anderson will give me all the drugs I want. He promised me he wouldn't let me be uncomfortable."

"I want you to go to Johns Hopkins or Mayo's or Duke. Carleton works at Duke. I'll call him. See what he suggests."

"Not this month. I need to get away, Charles. Go on a cruise. I want to make use of the time when I can walk."

"A cruise? To where?"

"To Egypt maybe. To see the pyramids. I want to leave

right away. This lasagna is great. I'd forgotten how much I love it. I craved it when I was pregnant. Do you remember that?" She reached across the table and took his hand. "Stop worrying. I'll tell you when I need you to worry."

LATER, WHEN THEY were getting ready for bed, he started it again. "We need to go to a great medical center and just see what they say."

"They'll say I'll be crippled soon. This is not a mysterious disease, Charles. They don't understand the causes but the progression is understood. Take a sleeping pill and go to sleep."

"Which one should I take?"

"Take the Clonazepam. I took one last week when my hands were bothering me. I slept for ten hours and didn't have a hangover. It's an old pill they don't prescribe much anymore."

"I don't take pills, Philipa. I'll just read awhile. Get in bed and read with me."

"Not now. I want to get on the computer and find a cruise to Egypt. I haven't seen the pyramids since Daddy took us when I was sixteen."

"I'll go wherever you want to go. I'll need a week or two to get things straight at the office. I'm helping Larry with a case. But I want us to get a second opinion and soon."

"It's not worth the time. Multiple sclerosis is understood. I've been watching my cousin David for years. It's probably genetic, another blue-eyed blond immune failing. Which is why I'm glad Caroline Jane is dating that Italian.

"Oh, my God. Come on, Philipa. Get in bed. We'll read and cuddle. I need you."

"In a while."

He climbed into the bed. He was wearing a faded pair of blue Brooks Brothers pajamas and he had an old cardigan around his shoulders. He picked up a stack of books from his bedside table and found the one he wanted. It was a spy novel by Daniel Silva. He opened the book to a scene where the Mossad agent named Gabriel was in the process of saving the life of the Pope. The scene took place in a synagogue in Rome where the Pope was about to make a speech apologizing for the Catholic Church's role in the Holocaust.

Philipa put the bottle of Clonazepam on the bedside table with a thermos of water. "In case you change your mind," she said. "We aren't going to get addicted to anything at our age, Charles."

"It's not cancer," he said. "It isn't life-threatening."

"It might as well be," she answered. "It threatens the way I live."

Charles watched her leave the room, her pink silk gown and robe trailing behind her. She still had beautiful posture, still walked like a dancer, still seemed in charge. Why a cruise, he wondered. Why not take our boat and sail in the Virgin Islands? Maybe she really does want to see the pyramids again, burial mounds where secret shafts of light connect the mummies to their gods. Hard to believe in God when you need him. Have to believe in the church, in the idea as a force for good; have to believe in something.

He closed his book and laid it on the bedside table. Then he got down on his knees and began to pray to the God he hoped somehow existed. "Now I lay me down to sleep," he began. "Don't let her die. Don't let her suffer, don't take her away from me. Tell me what to do. I don't know what to do. I don't know how to watch this happen to her." Then he was crying, his face in his folded hands.

After a few minutes he stood up and looked at the bottle of pills she had left on the table. He read the label. No, he decided. I'll just read.

"The Rome Central Synagogue: Eastern and ornate, stirring in restless anticipation. Gabriel took his place at the front of the synagogue, his right shoulder facing the *bimah,* his hands behind his back, pressed against the cool marble wall. Father Donati stood next to him, tense and irritable. The vantage point provided him perfect sight lines around the interior of the chamber. A few feet away sat a group of Curial cardinals, dazzling in crimson cassocks, listening intently as the chief rabbi made his introductory remarks. Just beyond the cardinals stirred the fidgety denizens of the Vatican press corps . . ."

Reading wasn't working. Philipa was up to something. He had not known her all these years without knowing her mind. Dr. Anderson had told him she would be in denial but she was not in denial. She was wide awake and planning. She had told him a thousand times she would never agree to be an invalid, never be in anyone's power, never die in a bed.

He picked up the bottle of pills and read the label again. He poured one out into his hand and put it into his mouth and swallowed it without water. Then he took the thermos of water and poured a glassful and drank it. Then he climbed back into the bed and started reading again.

"As the Pope finally rose to speak, a palpable sense of electricity filled the hall. Gabriel resisted the temptation to look at him. Instead, his eyes scanned the synagogue, looking for someone or something that seemed out of place . . ."

PHILIPA FOUND A cruise to Egypt leaving in three days time. Perfect. Charles would never be able to leave that soon. She'd tell him to meet her in Cairo, that she wanted to tour the new archaeological museum with her cousin Courtney, whose husband was a United States diplomat.

The cook came in early and made breakfast, fresh canta-
loupe, omelets, and toast made from homemade bread their
neighbor Callie had brought by the day before. The word
was out. This was not a secret anymore. Philipa had not
been able to hold a book at book club the month before and
she had seen a friend in the waiting room of the nuclear
medicine lab. "It's probably multiple sclerosis," she had told
him. "Two of my first cousins have it. It isn't bad yet."

"You're too old to develop that," the friend answered. "It's
probably arthritis. You should go further south for the winter. Cold weather makes my hands and knees hurt all the
time."

"We'll see," Philipa had answered. "We shouldn't have
gotten old, Jimmy. It was a big mistake. A really bad idea."

Charles came to the breakfast table dressed in a suit and
tie. She waited until he was finished eating before she told
him she was leaving. "I really have to get out of town for a
while," she said. "Too many people know about this and I
don't want to talk about it. There's a cruise leaving Cape
Canaveral at noon on Friday. I'm going to be on it. I'll wait
for you in Cairo. Courtney's there. I called her this morning. She's going to take me to the new museum. When you
get there we'll go down the Nile to see the pyramids. You've
never seen them, have you?"

"Why Friday? If you'll wait a week I'll go with you."

"I want to be alone for a while. I don't want to talk to anyone right now, even you, my darling. It's my disease. I need to think about it."

"You need to tell the children. They want to know what's going on. You need to talk to them."

"I'll talk to the children at Thanksgiving. When we're at the beach together. I don't want their lives shadowed by this. What good does that do?"

"What can I do to help you?"

"Nothing. I bought a ticket last night and got a flight to Cape Canaveral tomorrow. Maybe I'll gamble on the boat, dance with strangers, do karaoke." She was laughing now. She had made him smile. "I'm taking my laptop. I'm going to write it down, process it on paper, do research."

"Will you be all right?"

"I've got every drug known to man counting all the things they've been prescribing for arthritis. I'll have a swimming pool, hot tubs, people to wait on me hand and foot, people I don't know who aren't trying to decide what to say to me."

He folded his napkin and got up and went around the table and kissed her on the cheek.

"Go to work," she said. "I'm all right. I have a plan and I'm going to carry it through. Then I'll come home and go to Duke with you if that will make you happy."

• • •

IN THE FOUR Seasons Hotel in Cape Canaveral she dumped her cosmetic kit out on the bed and lined up the pills. Then she started reading the Physician's Desk Reference she had bought at Barnes and Noble. She had thirty 3-mg Lunesta, forty Ambien CR, and twenty-six Clonazepam. She had forty Percadan, a hundred oxycodone, ninety-seven Baclofen and fifteen Carisoprodol.

You drink two glasses of champagne, wait a few minutes, drink eight ounces of water, then start swallowing the pills. Oxycodone first, then Baclofen, then Ambien. That should do it. Maybe another glass of champagne.

Then you climb the railing, move around to a space clear of the engines, then jump or fall into the cold dark ocean. Don't think, don't panic, don't look back, don't whine or plead or care. Don't give in to fear. Fear is for illiterate children. You can't stay. You can't continue to live in the world as an effective person in a good mood. There is this one thing you have left to do and you can do it. Let the brainwashed, unread fools wait for death like slaves. Not me, not my father's daughter. Not my grandfather's gene-bearer. Fourteen grandchildren and a great-grandchild. I've done what I was here for.

SHE PUT THE pills in a leather purse and zipped it and put it into the bedroom safe. Then she dressed in a pale-peach-colored blouse with ruffled sleeves and an old pair of white linen pants and went down to the dining room and ordered dinner. She had salmon with crab sauce and french fried potatoes and flan for dessert. She ate as much as she could and then got up and walked out onto the patio to watch the stars. There will be stars to guide me, she decided. Twice this many on the ocean tomorrow night, great constellations, stardust, all we are, all we ever were or ever will be.

In the morning a driver picked her up and took her to the cruise ship and she was whisked through the first-class line and taken to a stateroom. "Not so much luggage," the Indonesian porter noted. "Very good not take much luggage."

She giggled and handed him two twenty-dollar bills. When he left she lay down on the bed to answer Charles's cell phone calls. "I'm writing it all down," she told him. "I'm pretending to be a reporter. When can you come? Have you made reservations?"

"If I fly Monday I'll be in Cairo before you get there. I don't know why you want to cross the Atlantic this time of year."

"To watch stars, of course, silly. I'm actually having a good time. I didn't know how nice it is to be alone."

"Peter called. They're having trouble with Peter G. The kindergarten teacher says he's acting up. Peter wants to know if they should look for a better school."

"Tell Peter to let Peter G. stay home one or two days a week. School is boring. Little children die of boredom in their terrible, boring schools."

"Will you call him?"

"No. I don't want to talk to them yet. Take care of it, Charles. Tell him what I said. Tell him five-year-old children shouldn't be shut up all day with their overworked teachers and equally bored siblings."

There were five other calls but she erased the messages without listening to them.

Then she went up on the deck and ate a bowl of chocolate ice cream and wandered down to the swimming pool to watch the people.

LATE THAT AFTERNOON she found the place. It was on the back of the boat behind a place that had been cleared for yoga classes. There was a folding laddered stool for the yoga teacher to sit on while she talked. It would do nicely to climb the railing. On the other side of the railing was a smooth, curved outcrop that she could move along to get to a space beside the motors.

• • •

THE NEXT MORNING Philipa woke early and went up on the deck to watch the early yoga class. She could still do some of the simpler moves, and when the teacher asked her to join them she did. There were only three other students, two middle-aged women and a girl who looked like a dancer. The music was Deva Premal, something Philipa had heard in yoga classes one wonderful summer when she did yoga every morning on the coast with an inspired teacher named Maya. The summer ended when Philipa's left hip and leg gave way beneath her and had to be treated with cortisone epidurals, but it remained a memory of a special time.

Philipa took great joy and pleasure from the class. It does not matter how long you live, she decided. It only matters that you love it while you're here.

In the afternoon she wrote beautiful long letters to her sons and daughter and to all of her grandchildren and great-grandchild. She wrote notes to her three closest friends, an apology to her cousin Courtney in Cairo, and a short letter to Charles.

Darling husband, heart of my heart. Allow me this surcease from suffering. I cannot be an invalid. I cannot be an old, sick, dying person. I have given you all my selfish heart has to give because your goodness and unselfishness called it from me.

Take care of the children. Give them advice but not too
much money. Charles II and William are independent.
And Caroline could be if she tried. She will hate me for
this. That will be useful to her in the end. But don't you
hate me. I'm setting you an example in case you need it.

Stay away from hospitals unless you want to die in one.
I love the doctors and nurses but they're too tired and they
have to lie. Nothing is of value except to have lived well
and to die without pain.

I love you, Philipa

At three the next morning she dressed in slacks and heavy,
laced-up boots and went up on the deck and walked back to
the yoga place. She had already swallowed an Ambien and
an oxycodone. When she got to the railing she drank half
of the bottle of champagne. She was feeling woozy but she
managed to climb over the railing and walk along the curved
surface still holding the champagne and the pills. She had not
thrown up yet. She did not feel like she was going to throw
up. That was good. The gods were with her. She swallowed
some more of the pills and stood holding the railing until she
thought they had begun to take effect. I was an athlete, she
told herself. I can do this. I can still hold on and I can let go.

She moved carefully along the curved edge and stopped
and looked up at the stars and acknowledged their magnifi-

cence. Then she took three woozy, unstable steps and fell. She saw the white light but it was not as brilliant as it was the time the car went off the mountain road in Wyoming in the snow or the time the company plane crashed in Virginia. Then she was cold, so very, very cold, and upside down in water, and then, mercifully, for there is a merciful god for those who want him, the water threw her into the motors and her brain stopped before she could gasp for air.

"SHE WAS ALWAYS lucky," her daughter, Caroline, told a psychiatrist several weeks later, after the confusion and disbelief and mourning had died down and people had gone home to their own lives. "She probably died before she could drown. Someone saw it from a high deck. They found enough of the body to know what happened. There were enough drugs in her stateroom to kill all the old people in North Carolina. She was so selfish, she never cared about anyone but herself. She never loved me. She could never quit saying what she thought about anything. Even if she managed not to say it, you knew she was thinking it. She thought I was a failure and she didn't like failure. She hated ugly people and she hated failure. I don't know how Daddy stood to be married to her."

"But you aren't a failure," the doctor said. "And you aren't selfish. You're like your father. You care about other people."

"I don't want to ever die." Caroline was crying now, curled up in a ball on his sofa with a box of Kleenex clutched in both her hands. "What sort of an example is it to do something like that? How will I ever die in peace when my own mother couldn't do it?"

"You aren't going to die for a long, long time," he said. "Let's don't keep dwelling on that now." He sighed, wanted so much to leave the room. No one dies in peace, he wanted to say, unless they are on morphine, which is not that much better than jumping off a boat.

"Let's stop for today," he told Caroline. "I think you've had enough. Will you start exercising again, for me? Exercise is so important now, Caroline. I hate to harp on it but it is vitally important right now."

"All right," she said. "I will. I'll do it to spite her, goddamn selfish bitch." She got up and put on her coat and collected her scarf and Prada bag and smiled at him and left.

He went to stand at the window that looked out on Touro Hospital, watched the crippled people being let out of cars and sent into the doors of the old, crippled hospital that was barely surviving since the hurricane.

He was trying to imagine a seventy-eight-year-old woman with the balls to jump into the Atlantic Ocean. It cheered him up to imagine it and he decided to go out and run six miles in the park in honor of her will and dominance and strength and concentration and disregard for what the world expects from us. She was probably like that all her life, he decided. What her daughter calls selfishness was there at the end to see her through.

Maybe her daughter has it, too, but I think not. She's made of thinner cloth. No wonder her mother didn't like her. I have a hard time liking her myself. I've stayed too long at this fair. I don't like them all anymore. Maybe I don't like any of them.

I could do research. Actually, I could just quit.

He got up and closed and locked his door and picked up the phone and told the receptionist to cancel his afternoon appointments. Then he went out the back door and down the stairs and went home and changed into running clothes and went to the park and ran six, seven, eight, nine miles and felt marvelous at the end.

A Love Story

This has to be recorded. He came to me last night and lay with me in the bed where for forty years I slept with another man and it did not matter. Nothing mattered. Not after many months of standing near me at the hospital while we worked to undo the damage life and craziness and disease cause other human bodies until our own were only vassals of the work we do. Every day for all those months I liked it when he was there and he liked it when I was there and we were helpful and invigorating for one another. Why did it surprise me when it came unto this other thing?

Biblical language is called for here if I am to get this down, to save this moment so I can think about it and believe in it and understand its moment and its power.

I am a mother of many children. I am not old because I move too much and work too hard and eat too carefully and am too vain. I was a beautiful girl and I am a beautiful older woman. I know that. So why was I surprised when he lay on me and our bodies began to give each other this blessing so powerful and perfected and sweet? I did not use my hands and he did not use his except to hold me against him when it was over. Our bodies found each other and made the long, sweet merging that would have made a baby in another time in our lives. I know when my babies were made. I know the difference in those nights and the other nice but not perfect matings.

This was the night that brings the egg to fruition and sends the sperm to brighten it into the future of our being. Yes, it was that good. I had not imagined wanting it again.

We still had on part of our clothes. He had on a white cotton T-shirt and the white shirt he brought back from Mexico when he went diving one last time, he said, but he has already planned another trip when winter comes.

When winter comes this town becomes so cold and gray, the leaves are gone, the wind comes down from Canada and ices the branches and prunes them. I am always preparing for it in November, like today, like I was yesterday, like now.

"I want to come by and bring you something I ordered for you," he said to me. Was that only yesterday afternoon? After work, when we were leaving the hospital and had walked out into the parking lot together. The leaves on the sugar maples are brilliant red and the sycamores are yellow and there is a hint of purple in the color, royal purple like the sweater I was wearing yesterday.

"What on earth?" I said.

"Ridiculous. I ordered it one night and it came and I want to give it to you. It's too large to bring to the hospital."

"Then come on. Come have supper if you like. It's lonely for me with my girls gone. I'd like to have an excuse to set the table. I live on Duncan Street . . ."

"I know where you live. I asked you once. Don't you remember?"

"Of course I do." I pulled my raincoat close around my body and pretended to be in a hurry.

"What time?" he called after me.

"Any time," I said. "Six o'clock is good."

He watched until I got into my car and started the motor and drove away. He always did that if he walked out with me. As if to protect me even when it was light. The way my father would stand in the driveway when I left my parents' house and would stand there until I was out of sight. People don't do that anymore for one another. A long time ago we didn't know how long it might be before we saw one another again. Or else we don't care as much or else we are distracted.

And so I set the table with pretty blue place mats and flowers and candles and Momma's Strasbourg silver and he came around six and we ate dinner early and he made me open the large package. It was some new sort of blanket that is very light and keeps the heat in. He had ordered it in pink. A large, pink, scientifically designed blanket he had ordered from the back of *Discover Magazine*.

"So you won't have to worry about electric blankets," he said. "You always say you are cold." He stood before me then, a man, a powerful, beautiful man who wanted to make love to me and has wanted that for more than a year and I knew it and I was too afraid to do a thing but stand there knowing I was not going to resist and also that I was not going to stop being terrified.

"I haven't done this in years," I said. "I don't think I know how. I don't think my body will do this. I'm too embarrassed to even know where to begin."

THEN WE WENT into my bedroom. We could have gone into a guest room. It didn't have to be mine and David's bed but I didn't think about that then and we lay down upon the bed fully clothed and began to neck like teenage children and after a while he pulled the covers down and we lay on the sheets and I took off my skirt and nylon hose, I don't remember how, and he took off some of his clothes but not the shirts and I reached my hand down to touch him but he took my hand away and climbed on top of me and our bodies found each other and gave each other meaning and great forgotten pleasure and he went deeper and deeper into me and it played out in waves like the sea and all that time he was the same man I see every day with the same thoughtful expression on his face and every move perfected because what he does and I do cannot be done any other way or people are harmed and die and so we concentrate on our work. It is a fierce profession full of blood and guts and terror and you become selfless or you cannot do it although some people do it anyway and no one who does it right is stupid enough to trust them.

Afterward we lay together in great quietness and finally he said, "I'm still hungry. Let's go get a steak somewhere. Peter will fix us something if I call him. Let's go down there."

I knew he was starving. The soup and bread I served him for dinner wasn't much and he had hardly eaten that since this was coming and we both knew it. I had no idea what time it was but it was probably about eight thirty. The restaurant he wanted to go to was only a few blocks away and he was right, they would have anything we wanted waiting for us. He is a powerful man who commands other men without moving or saying many words. And a good man and not a man who takes women and uses them. He is a gentleman and now we have been together in the strangest thing a man and woman can do. This love, this tenderness, this blessing.

"Go on," I said. "I don't want to go with you right now. I think we would be embarrassed to be in public with this right now. We might not know what to say."

"I will know. I want you to live with me, Annie. I have loved you since the day I saw you walking down the hall toward me. I know what I love. I loved my wife until she died and now I love you. I don't change my mind about something that important."

"What will people say?"

"They will wonder why it took so long for you to marry me."

"Marry me."

"On your terms, on any terms. Soon. I don't have long now, Annie. I can't waste what is left of my life. I want you to be there when I come home."

"And all day at work?"

"However you want. Whatever you want."

. . .

HE DID NOT get up and leave right away. He held me and whispered to me for a few more minutes and then he fell asleep. After a while I fell asleep, too, and when he woke he dressed and left and said he would call me in the morning and he did and now I have all day to think about this.

In the living room is the beautiful pale pink scientifically engineered Danish blanket he ordered for me out of *Discover Magazine*. In my heart is a sort of greatness and goodness I can't walk around or leave behind as I spend this day picking up a lamp I left to be repaired and maybe painting my toenails to match the blanket and maybe going to Whole Foods to get some food into this house and then what? At two o'clock I will drive out to the hospital and take a late shift for a friend and he will be there and yes, it will be okay because love is okay. Love is redeemable. You get your money back from love and you get to keep it, too. I think. I hope and pray.

Jumping Off Bridges
into Clean Water

The river was smooth and fast-moving because it had rained the night before. The storm had come in from the north and knocked down power lines all the way from Greenville to the Grace Post Office. It was 1944, and people knew what to do when that happened.

Even before the lights went out, Jimmy's great-grandmother got out six lanterns and set them in a line on the dining room table. She filled them with oil and lit them with long matches carved out of fat pine.

Jimmy took cushions from the porch furniture and carried

them into the front hall and then stood with his grandfather in the door to watch the rain watering the fields. They needed a new roof for the house. If the cotton made, they could buy asphalt shingles. If not, they would patch the roofs with long, flat tiles made of cypress. Jimmy had helped fell the big cypress tree they cut last summer. He had heard it fall and felt the soft delta earth shake beneath his feet as it did.

The night's rain had been enough to fill the river above which he was standing now, on the long silver bridge built by the WPA. Before the bridge was built you had to drive all the way around three plantations to get to Mayersville. Before it was built Jimmy's grandfather had to stand on his side and their neighbor, Mr. Anderson, stood on his and they yelled news to one another. Now they just went across the bridge to get to the Andersons' place or to Esperanza or Grace or on to Greenville.

JIMMY WAS ON the bridge with his cousins and the Anderson boys and their cousins. The river was deep and clear and fast-moving. Safe to jump. After you jumped from the bridge you could swim downstream to the pier at the store and climb up the ladder and shake the water from your hands and watch it fall in diamond shatters in the sun. You could wave to the bridge and watch the next boy jump.

You could watch him hesitate and gather his courage and then leap into the air.

It was summer and the rains had come, and there were enough boys on the two plantations to have baseball games in the pasture in the late afternoons and cut open watermelons and run races on the flat brown road and watch to see if the girls from Esperanza would come walking down the road in their blue and pink and yellow dresses. Sometimes, in daydreams, Jimmy would reach out and touch the dresses. When he was fifteen, he would go to cotillion dances and put his arms around a girl, but not yet. Although he had danced with Cecelia Alford at a wedding when he carried the ring and she was the flower girl. Her dress had felt stiff and fluffy, but underneath, her body was as soft as a flower and as alive and wild as his.

He didn't have to worry about Cecelia Alford now. All he had to do was stand on the bridge and wait for his turn to jump.

"What if you hit an alligator?" Jodie Myers whispered to him. Jodie was only ten years old. He said anything he thought up.

"What if I did?" Jimmy answered.

"You'd crack open your head."

"I would not. I'd knock that old gator to hell and back. Besides, there are no alligators in this river. Danny said so."

"There're snakes and gars."

"Then don't jump if you're afraid," Jimmy said. "But don't talk to me anymore. I'm thinking."

"About what?"

"About Cecelia Alford is what. I'm learning how to dance so I can dance with her. Miss Bodie is teaching me. I'm going to ask her if she wants to be in love."

"With which one? Miss Bodie or Miss Cecelia?"

"With both of them if I want to be. Go on, move up, it's almost your turn. And don't do any silly stuff. Just jump off and get out of my way."

Jodie stepped onto the pole in the center of the bridge and climbed halfway up and jumped into the river. It was an unremarkable jump but everyone cheered and clapped.

Jimmy climbed the pole. He climbed almost to the top, then hesitated. He looked down the road and saw the very edge of a blue and white dress with a white sash. It was Cecelia and her sister. Jimmy tore his eyes away and climbed to the top rung and spread his arms and dove into the river without looking. He sprang into the air and bent his body and dove. He was afraid of nothing and would have no need to be for many years.

When he surfaced he looked up at the bridge. The girls had come almost to the center and were looking down. Their tutor was with them, a young man from Ole Miss who played on the Ole Miss baseball team. He smiled and waved at Jimmy. Jimmy raised a hand and waved back, looking only at the tutor while he did. Then he stretched out his long, thin body and swam a perfect Australian crawl all the way to the pier at the store.

When he pulled himself up the ladder he turned his back to the bridge and walked into the store to borrow a shirt from his uncle. He didn't want Cecelia looking at his bony arms and chest. His uncle gave him an old white cotton shirt without asking why he wanted it. His uncle never asked questions.

"THIS RIVER RUNS into the Mississippi both underground and above ground," the tutor was saying to the crowd gathered around him at the edge of the bridge. "It's a meandering bayou, but down here it becomes a river. We're lucky to have it near so we can study the waterways of our county. I grew up in Yazoo City, and we used to go out on field trips to see how the Yazoo turns and curves and falls toward the Mississippi. Here we can see it right in our front yards."

Cecelia looked up at Jimmy and smiled without taking her eyes from him. She was a bold girl and always let him know she was glad he was there. It was all there, for anyone to see.

He took a deep breath, then walked to her side and looked down to where her hand lay on the cotton gingham of her white and blue dress. He started to reach out and take her hand. She would have let him. She might even be the one to do it. "We're going to have a watermelon party this afternoon," she said. "We came over to invite you all to come."

"What time?" he asked.

"At five o'clock," she said. "My uncles are going to demonstrate their new crop duster. We can watch them from the backyard."

"I'll be there," Jimmy said. "The river is so deep now," he added.

"I saw you jump," she said. "I wouldn't jump off that bridge for all the tea in China. I don't know why you all want to jump into the water."

"It's fun," he said. "When you're in the air it's really fun. And swimming to the pier with the river pushing you. It's like sailing in the water."

"Mr. Jenkins is drawing maps of the waterways near us," she said. "Come and look at what he's doing."

They walked over to the flattened rock where the tutor was drawing a sketch of the waterways of Issaquena County. He was a good draftsman and the map was clear and easy to read.

"We could take skiffs and go down these waters," he was

saying. "But we'd have to get off before we get to the Mississippi. The Mississippi is a great drain. It would suck a small boat in. There are tides and eddies that change all the time."

Jimmy wanted to say something to Cecelia but he didn't know how. He just kept on standing next to her wondering what it would be like to touch her hair. Her sun-filled hair that shone and moved in the slightest breeze and gave the world purpose and excitement and danger.

1975

It was an afternoon party in a house near Millsaps College, in Jackson. Jodie Myers was running for the Senate and had to be in Jackson for Democratic fund-raisers. He was forty-five years old and had decided to spend the rest of his life in public service. He had hired a manager to run his plantation and had thrown himself into running the race as he had always thrown himself into everything. "Thrust upon me by being the youngest boy on two plantations," he was saying to a woman who was standing so near to him he was about to have a coughing fit from her perfume.

"You always lived in Issaquena County?" she asked. "Since you were born?"

"My whole life, except for when they made me go to Culver Military Academy so I'd have the education I needed to go to Ole Miss. Everyone had to go off to school sooner or later. We didn't mind. Well, I minded being cold in the winter." He smiled at the woman and managed to move back a few steps.

"I know someone from there," the woman said. "My third cousin married a boy named Jimmy Peoples. Do you know him?"

"Jimmy was my idol growing up. When he was ten years old he picked up a cottonmouth moccasin by the tail and slammed it against a tree. He did it to save his uncle who was with him. It was ready to strike his uncle and he picked it up and killed it. Three people saw him do it, but he says he didn't do it on purpose. He always said that. He's a fine man."

"But then he got polio."

"After he married Cecelia. It wasn't a bad case. He can still walk, with crutches or a walker. He's lived a full life. He never stopped. He used to have his overseer drive him to Greenville four times a week to swim in the country club pool. His overseer would push his wheelchair right up to the pool and Jimmy would jump in and swim a mile. People would go see him, he got so good, so fast. When it was fall he would swim two or three miles to store up strength for winter. He's had a happy life."

"Well, he married a wonderful woman," the woman said. "My cousin never stopped loving him. That's not something you see much anymore, that kind of love, that kind of devotion."

"I see it," Jodie said. "I see it every day. I see it in all kinds of folks from all kinds of backgrounds. Love is devotion. Love is the choice you make and how you keep on making it no matter what happens."

"I wish I knew more of them," the woman said. "Those kinds of people. I want to be with them."

"Join my campaign," he said. "Come put yourself in their path. Do you have a job?" he looked at her designer suit and shoes and handbag. Of course she didn't have a job. "Are you married? Do you have children?"

"I want to," she said. "But I haven't yet."

"Come work for me. We have big things going on. We need all the help we can get. This is a big election."

"I might do that," she said. "I really might."

Later, his auditor told him he had been talking to the daughter of the biggest automobile dealer in the state. "She came over and signed up to help with fund-raising," the auditor said. "What did you do to her, Jimmy? She's starstruck."

"Her cousin married an old friend of mine. It's a happy marriage. I guess she thinks I know why."

"What did you say to her?"

"I told her there were heroes. I told her there were people who know how to love."

1992

"I'm not going to live forever, Cecelia," Jimmy was saying. "You have to face that and pay attention when I show you things. The children will need you to take care of all this. It's only an insurance policy on the place in Issaquena County. It's not a death certificate. It's what has to be taken care of so I can die in peace when the time comes."

"I can't talk about it, Jimmy. Let Butch take care of it. He's our lawyer. Why should I have to read everything?"

"Because you have to know exactly what to do so you won't be confused. These are the details of the fruits of the labors of three generations of men and women."

"John Wilson said you were fine when we talked to him last month. He said you were doing well."

"I'm doing well for someone with one lung that works forty percent of the time. You'll be young when I'm gone. I want you to travel. I want you to get married again."

"Stop!" She turned furiously toward him. "Don't talk to me like that." She went out the front door and down the long path to the garden and put on her gloves and began to savagely pick at her rosebushes. Then she got out the poison and began to spray the bushes. He was going to do it and soon. I know him, she decided. He won't be a complete invalid. There's no way he will stay for that. He thinks he can make up for it by having all the papers in order and no bills outstanding and all the taxes paid. I know what he's doing. He'll go off somewhere in the deadening and do it with a pistol. I know how he thinks. I know who he is.

He came walking up behind her. He was using the walker. He never used the wheelchair except on very bad days. It was amazing how tall he had remained.

"Let's go into Greenville and have dinner at Doe's and see a movie," he said. "I put away the papers. Stop being mad and go into town with me."

She turned and pulled off her gardening gloves and fell for it in spite of herself, as she always fell for it.

"All right," she said. "But swear you will stop writing wills in the middle of the summer."

"I'm finished anyway," he said. "And you don't have to read it if you don't want to."

She moved near to him and reached out and touched the powerful arm that still allowed him to hold himself upright. "Let's go change clothes," she said. "I'm not going into town looking like this."

Cecelia changed into a pale yellow sundress with a brilliant yellow scarf around the waist for a belt. She took off her sandals and put on two-inch-high white platform shoes she had polished that morning in a fit of old-fashioned perfectionism.

Oh, go on and dress up, she told herself. He loves for you

to be pretty. She put on her mother's pearls and pearl earrings and two gold bracelets her grandmother had given her on birthdays.

Jimmy was waiting when she came onto the side porch. "A vision," he said. It was something he'd read once in a book and it always worked. Cecelia grinned like a girl and let him put his arm around her and steer her out the door and down the two steps into the waiting car. He kept one hand around her waist and another on his cane and somehow managed all this without it seeming labored.

They drove out the long, packed gravel driveway to the two-lane asphalt road that curved around the fields of picked cotton and past the Indian mounds they had played on as children. They came to Highway 1 and turned northwest onto its shining four lanes of concrete and drove toward Greenville.

The air was cooling in the late afternoon, the sun was setting behind the levees, and the only sounds were crickets and late-afternoon birds. They passed the mile of catfish ponds Jimmy had built twenty years before with the help of a neighbor farmer. The ponds were ringed with white herons, standing on one leg waiting to feed again on the treasure of captive catfish.

"Don't you love to see the herons?" Cecelia asked. "I can't believe how you build something one day for one purpose and a week later there are hundreds of herons using it for a pantry."

"What else don't we know," Jimmy answered. "Or expect to happen. Something we can't imagine falls from the sky every time we turn around and there you are, new challenges, new paths to take, new decisions to be made."

"Well, I'll tell you one thing. If you get it into your head to go to the deadening and kill yourself with a gun or hang yourself like Mr. Allen did on Hopedale, then I will kill myself the next day, too, without bothering to bury you or burn you up in the cremator's oven or do a thing to help your children or grandchildren cope with losing you. That's a promise, Jimmy, so you can believe it. So be sure and get all those papers right for them."

Cecelia looked straight ahead, down the long four-lane highway, her chin set, her hands folded primly in her lap. She had said it and she was glad she had said it.

Jimmy pulled the BMW convertible off onto the side of the highway and turned off the motor.

"Sure I think about it," he said. "Who wouldn't?" She still would not look at him. "But I will not do it. No matter how bad it gets or how much I am a useless mind lying in bed with no body to do my will." He started laughing. "Like one of those space navigators in *Dune,* except I'll be in a bed instead of a tank of liquid and I'll be doing Demerol and morphine instead of spice. I might shoot myself in your bed and get blood all over your grandmother's sheets and bedspread, but I will not go out into the deadening and I sure won't hang myself. I promise you that."

She was laughing, too. She couldn't help herself. She was letting him get her tickled just like he always did if she tried to talk to him about something serious like when Little Jimmy started smoking marijuana or when he gave his friend Jodie five thousand dollars for his senatorial campaign.

"If you get blood on my Grandmother Tellie's linens from Paris I will get blood on your hunting guns and your first editions of William Faulkner's books and your autographed copy of Willie Morris's first book and everything else of yours in the house. I'll shoot myself and then I'll walk around the house getting blood on everything you like."

"How about I go to that clinic in Switzerland you and your buddy Courtney think can make me well. What if I take you late this fall and we go to Switzerland and stay two weeks and let these alternative medicine doctors you believe in try out all their quasi-scientific tricks on me. If I do that, will you let me go hunting at Christmas with Jodie and the governor and the crowd that are going from Texas?"

"At least I said it," she said. "At least I don't have to go around thinking it. You'd really go to Switzerland?"

"How much does it cost?"

"I'm going to pay for it out of my money Daddy left me. You will never know how much it cost."

"I said I'd go. Now stop thinking all those trashy suicide thoughts and let's go to Doe's and eat. Get them on the cellular phone and tell them we are coming and that I want the center table by the picture window. They know which one."

Jimmy pulled Cecelia over as near as he could what with the damned center console in the convertible. He hugged her and seriously kissed her, then he turned on the motor and put the top down and turned on the CD player to a CD of John Coltrane playing "My Favorite Things" and held his back up straight and drove on into Greenville. He was thinking about what it was like to lie in bed on his back and have her climb on top of him and make him come. Okay, he'd go to the alternative medicine clinic in the Alps and at least he'd get to see some spectacular scenery. If it didn't work then he had to think of a way to do it that really seemed like an accident, or maybe murder. It was going to be hard as hell to do because she was on the scent.

She was on the phone talking to the manager at Doe's.

"We can have that table if you have to have it," she said when she hung up. "Because it's a weekday but don't be surprised if we have to wait a few minutes when we get there. Bobby said your friend Jodie Myers was there with a woman from Jackson. He said she was very pretty. Hurry up, I want to see who he brought to Doe's."

"I know who it is," Jimmy said. "He told me about her last week. She's your third cousin from Jackson, the daughter of Ben and Rivers Luckett. She's lived in Mexico for the last seventeen years and just came home to Mississippi." He turned and looked at Cecelia, then drove faster toward the town.

"Jodie told me about it last week," he went on. "They met years ago, but she moved away. She likes him because he knows you and me. She says we're legendary for having a happy marriage. She heard I was the best crippled swimmer in Mississippi, and, besides, she's your cousin."

"I know that. So she thinks we have a happy marriage?" Cecelia was laughing again. "Wait until I tell her about your threat to get blood on Grandmother Tellie's embroidered sheets and pillowcases. I don't know why I even let you sleep on those sheets. Well, if you really go to Switzerland I might decide to be happy with you."

Jimmy pulled into the parking lot of the original Doe's Eat Place. He got out of the car and came around and opened the door for Cecelia. "Be on your best behavior," he told Cecelia. "Marrying Angele Luckett might be the thing that puts Jodie in the Senate. Then we can go to Washington and sit up in a balcony and watch him preen around on the Senate floor."

He took her arm in one hand and his cane in the other and they went up the two steps and onto the screened-in porch and entered the restaurant. Jodie and Angele saw them and waved them over.

"SO YOU'VE JUMPED on Jodie's bandwagon," Jimmy began, being so charming Cecelia started getting jealous. "We need you. We need a U.S. senator from the delta. You can't educate these people unless you speak their language and understand them. Jodie's one of them. He took a servant with him to Ole Miss, did you know that? He did. I swear he did. His accent used to be so thick the only people he could talk to were field hands. And this is not a racist thing. He's the farthest thing from a racist you can find. You watch. He'll be the finest senator this state has ever had."

"He said I could be his education advisor," Angele said. "I'll be good at it. I was raised on a cotton plantation. I taught in our school when I was sixteen. I taught the young people how to read. I know how to get it done."

"Angele's a serious woman," Jodie said. He put a serious expression on his face. "So how are you, Jimmy? Are you doing well?"

"I am doing as well as anybody can that has to watch Ole Miss play that crazy schedule they have for them. Have you seen that fullback Mississippi State got from Yazoo City?"

"Let's order," Cecelia said, pulling her chair over closer to her cousin Angele. "I want to look at that jacket," she told her. "I haven't been anywhere to shop in two years. I'd forgotten what beautiful fabrics feel like. The only clothes I have are mailed to me by Maison Weiss and I can't even get to Jackson to have them altered properly. Where do you live, Angele? I heard you were in Africa or somewhere."

"I'm moving back to Jackson. To help run Jodie's campaign. Come and visit me and we'll get things altered at Maison Weiss."

"They're going to talk football all night."

"I think so. Jodie said they used to jump off a bridge into deep water all the time. He said it's a wonder they didn't put out their eyes."

"Men," Cecelia said.

"Men," her cousin answered. "Well, I like them."

"Me too," Cecelia giggled. "At least you have someone to feel superior to if you keep one around."

"I heard that," Jimmy said. "If I was someone who wanted to drag someone to Switzerland to have alternative medicine gurus poke and starve and pry on him, I'd be careful of my mouth in public."

Hopedale, A History
in Four Acts

I

One morning in the first year of the twentieth century, when Issaquena County had only begun to be cleared of trees, a little girl named Margaret was playing in a pile of sand when she saw a wagon come creeping across the bridge and turn onto the road to the house. The wagon was filled with black people. Two grown people on the seat and many children in the back.

Margaret stood up and watched the wagon move along the road. When it passed the fence that separated the yard from the pasture she waved and the children waved back. Margaret ran across the yard and up the steps to the porch. "Some people are coming," she told her mother. "A lot of them."

"From the floods," her grandmother said. Her grandmother was sitting in front of a sewing machine making a curtain. They had only lived in the house one year and they weren't through fixing it up yet.

"Let's go and see who it is," her mother said. She straightened her hair with her hands as she moved across the verandah and opened the screen door and went out onto the steps. The wagon had stopped twenty feet from the house and a tall man with a gray beard had climbed down and was walking toward them. He was a very thin man and he carried his hat in his hand. Margaret's mother waited for him to approach and let him speak first.

"We come from Deer Creek," the man began. "Where the floods are happening."

"Do you need food?" Mrs. McCamey asked. "We can feed you."

"No, ma'am. We need to leave a boy somewhere. He lost his folks in the flood and we can't keep him. We're going to Anquilla to stay with my auntie. We can't take any more than the ones we got."

"What kind of boy? How big is he?"

"He's a good boy. He's eight years old. Eli," he called to the wagon. "Get down and come over here."

A boy Margaret's size climbed down from the wagon and came to stand beside the man. He was a clean little boy, wearing a blue-and-white-checked shirt and some overalls. His face looked like a place where nothing had happened for a long time. He stood quietly beside the man, not moving, his hands folded in front of him.

"He's not sick," the man said. "He's a good worker. They worked over on Panther Burn Plantation. It's all flooded now. The house is gone. His momma and daddy were good people. They worked for Mr. Cortwright."

"Where are you from, son?" Mrs. McCamey asked. "Where were you born?"

"Up by Deer Creek on Panther Burn," he answered, looking her right in the eye. "I helped in the kitchen. I can make mayonnaise and I can churn."

"Are you hungry?" It was Margaret's grandmother talking now. She had come down from the screened-in porch and was taking over.

"Yes, ma'am," he said. "I could eat."

"You all go and sit at that table under that tree," her grandmother said. "We'll send someone out with cornbread and molasses. Margaret, go tell Baby Doll to bring food out for these people. Let me talk to the boy," she told the man.

"Come on, boy. Come here and let me see about you. What is your name?"

"Eli Naylor, ma'am," he said. "My name is Eli Naylor."

"You say you can make mayonnaise?"

"Yes, ma'am. I can hold the oil and drip it while my momma beats it. And I can churn and make butter and sweep the porches with a broom."

"Could you stay here if we keep you? You won't get lonely and run away?"

"I have to stay somewhere," he answered. "I have to have a place to be."

"Then leave him here," she said to the man. "Do you know how to write?"

"I can write."

"Then I'll give you a piece of paper with our mailing address on it and you can send word of where you'll be when you get to Anquilla. How much is flooded on Deer Creek?"

"Everything is washed away from Panther Burn to Mr. Charlie Larkin's place. The Red Cross came and helped some people leave. They gave us food and quinine for the children. Eli's had quinine every day. I don't think he'll get sick. I can leave some of it for him."

"No, we have it. You save what you have for your children. Come on over to the table now. You eat, then you get on to Anquilla before night comes. The mosquitoes get bad after dark along the bayou."

"You all is lucky the bayou didn't flood back here. What do you call this bayou?"

"Steele Bayou is its name."

"It's Lucky Bayou, is what it is." He followed his children and his wife to the wooden table under the huge old sycamore tree and they ate cornbread and molasses and drank cooled tea and then they took their leave of Eli and climbed back into the wagon and rode off down the road and across the bridge. Eli stood beside the fence waving at them until they were out of sight. Then he followed Margaret into the house and through the parlors and back into the kitchen where he would live for the next seventy years.

This was in the old times, in the time of floods and malaria and yellow fever and starvation, when the Mississippi Delta was being tamed and made into a place where men could live.

II

In the 1950s there had been three weddings in four years. Three times they had decorated the parlors and the verandah and the halls and set up tables with linen cloths and napkins and polished the silver and filled the candlesticks with candles and brought the Episcopal priest up from Rolling Fork and married off the girls. First Margaret, then Aurora, then Roberta.

Now they were having funerals. First Mr. McCamey, then

Dr. Finley. That was all the men they had, except for Guy, who was in school at Mississippi State. They had the husbands of the girls, but they all lived away, in New Orleans and Indiana. The McCamey men had been dying young ever since Margaret's grandparents had come down the Mississippi River in rafts and built the town and the church and the plantations. They had died of yellow fever and malaria from being on the river building levees. Now they were dying of cancer from being in the fields with the DDT they used to kill the boll weevils. The black people weren't dying of cancer yet. Only the white men were dying. The black people would die of it later, but the white men were first.

When Dr. Finley couldn't stand his pain he took morphine and went to sleep. When Mr. McCamey couldn't stand his he went out into the yard and hung himself from a tree that looked out across the bayou. He did it in the early morning so Man would find him when he came in at dawn. It was Man who had to cut him down and go up to the house and tell the women what he'd found. Man was six feet seven inches tall. When he got through telling the women and seeing that the body was taken into town to the undertaker, he went to the store and had Mr. Cincinnatus sell him a bottle of whiskey and then he saddled a horse and rode up the Deadning and sat out in the field he and Mr. McCamey had cleared when they were young and he walked around among the small, early-summer cotton and drank all the whiskey and cried and thought about Mr. Mac swinging in the wind like a sail, just swinging a little bit in his suit pants and shirt and tie still tied around his neck.

"It's the poison they been putting on the plants," Baby Doll told him, when Mr. Mac got sick. "It's all that poison. I told you to wash it off your face and hands when you be moving it. It's got that bad smell. You need to wash it off when you come in from spraying it."

"We're going to be spraying it from an airplane soon," Man had told her. "Mr. Bubba Wade is fixing that old plane he's got up on his place so he can fly on top of the fields and spray it on and we don't have to carry it no more."

"Who's going to run this place now?" Baby Doll asked after the last funeral was over. "Now all the men is dead except Guy and he's too young to run it. He's in Starkville."

"He can come on home. Me and Mr. Mac wasn't that old when we started Esperanza. I wasn't much older than Guy is."

"Guy could run it," Baby Doll said. "But they don't want him to. They want him to play football."

"Then Miss Nellie and Miss Margaret got to run it. Mr. Wade can tell them what to do. And I will run it like I always do."

"You can't write. You got to write to run it. You should have gone in the school when they had the teacher here."

"They didn't have the school. We didn't build it until after we built the store and I was grown by then." Man walked away from Baby Doll and went back up to the store to talk to Mr. Cincinnatus because he didn't like to talk about who knew how to write and who didn't know how. He was the strongest man in Hopedale. He didn't need to write anything down. He needed to get someone to drive into Rolling Fork and get some parts so he could fix the plow on the tractor. He needed Mr. Cincinnatus to close the store and get the parts and some engine oil for the engine.

ELI NAYLOR WAS sixty years old when the men died. Aurora's husband, Mr. Dudley, came down from Indiana and paid off the debts on Hopedale and put a new roof on the house and stayed a week going over the books and paying bills.

"Can you take care of these women now?" he asked Naylor.

"I'll do the best I can."

"Do you have a gun?"

"We got Mr. McCamey's guns in the case."

"You got people you can depend on?"

"I got Man and I got Sears and we got Mr. Cincinnatus at

the store. Miss Margaret's got her pistol but we don't need it. No one's coming on Hopedale to hurt us, is they?"

"Okay. Okay, then. Guy won't be home for two years. He has to finish his education. It's going to be up to you, Naylor. You have to be the man."

"I'll do the best I can."

"You call me if you need me. You know how to use the telephone?"

"I can use it if I have to. I know how."

"All right. All right then. I got to get back to my job, Naylor. I got to go home tomorrow. It's up to you now."

AFTER MR. DUDLEY left, Miss Margaret came into the kitchen and looked things over. "We have to clean out that cupboard, Naylor," she said. "We'll get weevils if we let it go."

"We been throwing everything in there. We had so many funerals we don't know what's going on. Abigail and Juliet were in there all the time eating cake when they were here."

They pushed the table and chairs out of the way and started taking things off the shelves in the cupboard.

"Go get that paint out of the garage," Miss Margaret said. "We need to paint these shelves before we put things back on them." She pulled a shelf board out into the light and Naylor took it from her and laid it on a chair. Then he went

out the door to the hall and down the hall to the porch and
down the porch stairs to the garage and started looking for
the paint.

III

November 1968. Hopedale Plantation, Issaquena County,
Mississippi. It was three in the afternoon and the mail car-
rier's truck had come and gone two hours before but Naylor still wouldn't go to the store and get the check unless
Margaret went with him and that meant they both had to wait
until Miss Nellie had time to drive them in the Buick. Naylor
walked to the store every day except the day the checks came,
but Margaret never walked to the store because it got her
shoes dusty and gnats came up from the bayou and got into
her hair. There were no gnats in November and no mosquitoes either. The only bugs left to see were a few large grass-
hoppers in the picked field that had been the pasture when
Mr. Floyd was alive and there were riding horses.

It was four thirty when Miss Nellie finally got up from
her nap and straightened her hair and put powder on her
face and told Sugar to get the car and bring it around to the
front door.

"Come on then," she told her mother. "Let's take him
down there."

Margaret took off her house shoes, which were all she

wore now because shoes hurt her corns. She put on silk stockings that she had fixed with elastic so they stayed up under her dress and slipped her feet into the uncomfortable leather shoes. She straightened her back and walked out onto the porch to wait for the car. Naylor came out from the kitchen to join her.

"It is a check," Margaret told Naylor for the tenth time that year. "No one can use it for anything until you sign your name to the back. It's only a piece of paper until you sign your name to it."

He was silent. He wasn't going to argue with her because he had been arguing with her for sixty years and he knew it did no good.

"This is ridiculous," Miss Nellie said. "You walk to the store every afternoon unless the check is there. It is only a quarter of a mile to the store. You can see the store from here."

"I needed to get some cinnamon anyway," Margaret told her. "It's all right."

Sugar drove up with the Buick and opened the doors for them. "I could drive you down there," he offered.

"No, I'll do it." Miss Nellie slid her five feet two inches into the driver's seat. She could barely see over the steering wheel because Sugar had moved her pillow so she got back out and they found the pillow and arranged it on the seat and she got in again and her mother got into the front passenger's seat and Naylor got into the back and Sugar closed the doors for them and Miss Nellie started the engine and they drove along the gravel road that led from the house past the pasture and beside the bayou to the store.

"I might as well get some gasoline while we're here," Miss Nellie said, and stopped the Buick beside the gasoline pump that stood between the store and the schoolhouse. Naylor got out of the backseat and opened the door for Margaret and then the door for Miss Nellie and they all went into the two-room store, which was run by Margaret's grandson, Cincinnatus, whose father had died when he was small.

"You all come to get the checks?" he asked, although he knew it was why they were there.

"Yes, he's going to sign his and we want you to take it to Rolling Fork to the bank," Miss Nellie said. "I'll put Momma's in my account when I go in on Monday."

"I could take them both," Cincinnatus offered. "Unless you're going in anyway."

He walked over to the mailboxes and took out two letters from two separate boxes and handed them to Miss Nellie.

"Tell him about the quarters," Naylor said.

"He wants a roll of quarters for the slot machine," Margaret said. "Give them to him now."

Cincinnatus opened the cash register and took out a

roll of quarters and handed them to Naylor and then they opened the government envelopes and took out the checks. Margaret signed hers and handed it back to Cincinnatus and then Naylor signed his and handed it to him. Margaret's check was for three hundred and ten dollars and Naylor's check was for three hundred and seventeen dollars. No one knew why the difference was there and no one had ever questioned it.

"We need some Wesson oil," Naylor said. "There isn't an inch left in the can."

"I only have it in the half-quart jar," Cincinnatus said. "Take that until we get in some more." He reached up on a shelf and got the oil, and then Margaret found the cinnamon and Nellie took down a bag of ground coffee and they set all the things on the counter and Cincinnatus rang it up and made a bill and Miss Nellie signed it and then Cincinnatus walked them to the car and filled it with gasoline and put them all in their seats and waved as they drove back toward the house.

"It's ridiculous to make Momma go to the store every time your check comes," Miss Nellie was saying to Naylor. "Just because Man and Baby Doll filled your head with that mess."

"Leave him alone, Nellie. It doesn't hurt me to go to the store. It's all right, Naylor. I wanted to get cinnamon anyway."

"We got to have it before all them come down here at Thanksgiving," Naylor said. "Is Miss Zell going to be here?"

"Don't you all change the subject," Miss Nellie said. "I don't mind driving you down there but you can't go on believing a pack of lies. The government sends you the checks because they passed a law in Washington to take care of old people who have worked all their lives. They are not mad at anyone because they have to do it. No one is going to hurt you because you sign the checks."

"Miss Zell went to a lot of trouble to sign us up for this," Margaret added. "It is called Social Security and Zell had to fill out a lot of forms and write letters so the checks come. All the old people are getting them, not just in the delta but all over the United States. If the government wanted to harm the people who get them they would have to harm thousands and thousands of people."

"We're going to have to get them turkeys early this year," Naylor said. He was tired of listening to them tell him about the checks. He knew all he needed to know about the checks. "Last year I never did get them thawed out after they'd been in the freezer up at Mr. Coon's. How many of them are coming to Hopedale this year?"

"I'm not going to talk about it anymore," Miss Nellie said "I've had my say. You can either believe me or believe a pack of lies Man told you to make a fool of you. He knows what he told you isn't true."

THEY ARRIVED AT the house and got out of the car and went up the steps, and Naylor and Margaret went into the kitchen to start supper and Miss Nellie went to her bedroom and lay down on her bed to finish reading her magazine. She had hardly gotten settled into a story when the telephone rang and she had to get up and go to the table to answer it. It was her daughter in New Orleans calling to tell her that her husband had been asked to go on a trip to Russia with the president of the United States and she was going, too. "What's going on at Hopedale?" the daughter asked, when she was finished telling her news. "What have you all been doing?"

"The same thing we always do," her mother answered. "Naylor believes the government is coming to Issaquena County to drown all the old Negroes in the bayou so they won't have to pay them Social Security, and Momma won't make him stop believing it, so we have to drive him down to the store to sign the check. She babies him so much."

"What does he do with the money?"

"We made him a bank account in Rolling Fork in case he gets sick and has to go to the hospital. It's about two thousand dollars now. Zell started all this. She filled out the forms."

"Well, I have to go now," the daughter said. "We're going to dinner with the Charbonnets. I'll talk to you on Sunday. Bunky and Sharon will be here. We'll call you then."

MISS NELLIE'S OLDEST daughter hung up the phone and went to her dresser and started fixing her makeup. It was getting harder and harder to call Hopedale and talk to them. It was her home and she missed it and she loved her mother and her grandmother, but there was nothing to do for them. Their lives were winding down and they didn't like to come to New Orleans anymore and stay with her. They wanted everyone to come to them and she was too busy to go down there all the time. She called her younger sister to talk to her about it. "We're going for Thanksgiving," she said. "We need to get them down here so we can take them shopping and get Grandmother some shoes, but they never want to come. Maybe they'll come back with us after Thanksgiving. There's no reason they have to be there that time of year. Coon Wade's farming the place."

"We'll take some shoes down there when we go," her sister suggested. "I'll call Grandmother and find out the sizes."

"We need to take her to a good foot doctor. They should come to New Orleans, but they don't want to do it."

"They went to Jackson last month to stay with Aurora. Dudley sent a car for them. We should send a car."

"I'll ask them when I talk to them on Sunday."

"I wish we could do more for them."

"We do all we can. They don't want us to do things for them. They are used to doing things for us. They're already getting ready for Thanksgiving. Is Nelson going hunting with the men this year?"

"I guess he is. I don't particularly want him to."

They were silent. They had both lost a son, one to a drunken driver, and one to an accident with anesthesia during surgery. They knew the world was full of danger and uncertainty and they could not forget it. Their sister in Jackson had never lost a child. She was still light-hearted, but they would never be light-hearted again, no matter how much they pretended that they were.

Miss Nellie got back up on her bed and went back to reading the story in *Good Housekeeping* magazine. It was about a girl in Nebraska whose young husband died in the Second World War. She remarried and had three children. Then she got a letter from Germany. Her first husband wasn't dead. *To be continued.* Miss Nellie closed her eyes and tried to imagine what she would do under those circumstances. Well, she would find out next month. *Good Housekeeping* came the first week of each month. This one had just come a few days before. They shouldn't have these continued stories, Miss Nellie decided. This was too much waiting.

In the kitchen Margaret and Naylor were arguing about when they were going to start making the cheese straws for Thanksgiving. Then they started arguing about the turkeys. "If you leave them out too long they can spoil," Margaret was saying. "Dr. Finley said if you freeze them and then thaw them out you have to cook them until there is no red anywhere and that's too dry. They get listeria if they sit too long. People can die from it."

"We need to get some turkeys that never are frozen and put in that freezer at Mr. Coon's place to begin with," Naylor said. "I'd rather have chickens than have to have these frozen ones. You can't get the dressing in them right."

"Well, that's what we have now. You have to be in the modern world, Eli. It's the modern world now and that's where we live."

"If we had some chickens we could make a nice dinner when they come."

"Well, we don't have chickens and turkeys come frozen from the store and that is what we are going to cook and that is that."

Margaret was sitting at the wooden table with a cup of coffee in a gold-banded cup that had been Nellie's wedding china. Naylor was sitting on his chair by the door. On the first night he had ever slept in Hopedale, Margaret's mother had made him a pallet on the floor beside the door so he could feel the heat coming in from the back fireplace and he had kept his chair there ever since. It was his place. He had a cup of pot liquor and cornbread in his hand and he was tasting it while he talked to Margaret.

"When those potatoes are finished cooking I'll make some potato salad," he said. On the stove a pot of potatoes was boiling and he was watching them.

"You better not let those potatoes cook too long," Margaret said. "They'll fall apart if you don't get them out on time."

"I know when to get them out," he said. "Look out there, Miss Maggie, it's getting so dark."

"It gets dark early this time of year," she answered. "It's November. That's what happens. We are moving farther away from the sun. Then on December twenty-first we start moving back toward summer."

"I hope we do," Naylor said. "I don't like it to get cold and dark."

"Well, it does. That's how it happens."

They were thinking about the darkness of November but then Sugar came in and started talking to them. "I got the hose and washed the dust off the Buick," he said. "Now I'm going home. You all want me to make a fire in the dining room before I leave? We got a pile of good firewood out back. I could bring some in. When Mr. Floyd was alive he always wanted a fire in November."

"That would be very kind of you," Margaret said. She

stood up and ignored the pain in her feet and started toward the dining room to help with the fire. Naylor put down his pot liquor and went to work on the potatoes.

In a while a beautiful fire was burning in the dining room and Margaret began getting out the china and place mats for their supper.

The phone started ringing. Margaret went back into the kitchen and took down the receiver and answered it. It was Aurora calling from Jackson. "You all getting along all right?" she asked.

"We're very well, my darling girl. Naylor's making hot potato salad and Sugar's building us a fire."

"Margaret's worried about your feet. I want to come and get you and bring you up here to a doctor. Could I come do that next week one day?"

"There's nothing wrong with my feet. Is everything all right with you, Sugar Pie?"

"I think you're wearing the wrong size shoe, Babbie. I want to take you to a man who can fix some of the corns and get you some shoes that fit. Margaret's worried to death about it and I told her I'd come see about it."

"Then come on down. We could take Naylor, too. He could use some new boots. He has two thousand dollars in the Farmer's and Merchant's bank now. From his Social Security checks."

"I will come down on Wednesday then. Write it down so you don't forget."

"Come on then, honey. I can't wait to see you and hold you by the hand. We'll be waiting for you."

Margaret hung up the phone and said a little prayer of thanks. Then she turned to Naylor, who had been waiting to see who was calling. "Aurora's coming on Wednesday to take us to the shoe store," she told him. "So get Sudie to give you a haircut and get all those hairs off your chin before she gets here. Tomorrow we'll have to find Baby Doll and get the parlors dusted. Don't cut those potatoes up so small, Eli. They soak up too much mayonnaise when the pieces are that small. And don't forget to put some celery into it. Nellie likes a lot of celery in hers."

She walked over to the refrigerator, refusing to pay attention to the pain in her feet, and opened the door and got out the celery and took it to the sink and started cleaning it.

"I know how to cut up potatoes," Naylor muttered, just loud enough for her to hear, but not loud enough to solicit an answer. "I guess I been cutting up potatoes without any help from anybody since I was by my momma's skirts on Panther Burn." And he went on cutting, not giving in to the sadness of thinking about his momma and times of long ago that were all dead and gone.

• • •

THERE ARE PLACES on Hopedale Plantation where the topsoil is thirteen feet deep. Cotton will grow there and soybeans and if you want to make a vegetable garden, you just turn the soil a little bit and throw down the seeds. You can turn your back and when you return there will be tomatoes and corn and green beans and bell peppers and okra and every kind of weed and grasshopper and caterpillar and earthworm and roly-poly and ant and wasp and dirt digger known to man and, in June, butterflies and moths and anything else you need to have plenty to look at if you get tired of talking to any people who are around.

IV

It was another November when Margaret fell on the floor in the back hall and the ambulance came and took her to the hospital in Greenville and all the girls started driving there from all over but only two of them got there in time to hold her by the hand and talk to her. Roberta had been away on a trip to New Mexico with her husband and only got there in the middle of the night, when it was already over.

The family came and there was a service in the Episcopal Church with the new young minister from up in Ohio reading the service in a nice, clipped manner.

Then they drove out to Greenfield's Cemetery and buried her in the shadow of the church her father and her uncles had built beside her mother's grave and the graves of all three of her mother's husbands, all of whom had been fathers to her and loved her and helped her in every way.

Naylor stood way back behind the family and wouldn't let anyone talk to him about it although he did agree to ride back to Hopedale with Aurora and her husband and Miss Nellie.

He didn't want to talk to anyone about it, even Mr. Dudley, who was always good to talk to about anything. He wanted to think about Margaret up in the clouds walking around on things so soft nothing would ever hurt her feet again and he was wondering what she had to eat up there and if they had anything to eat or if they just had to be hungry even if it was in heaven.

"Miss Babbie's at the Pearly Gates by now," Mr. Dudley was saying to cheer up the car. "She's probably through the gates and being fitted for her robes and harp."

"Can she see us, you think?" Naylor asked, being drawn in against his will. "What you think they eat up there, Mr. Dudley?"

"They have ambrosia and nectar," he said. "That's what my momma told me they had."

"They have anything they want, but they don't want anything," Aurora added. "People don't get hungry in heaven, Naylor. They are too busy thinking about other things."

"How you know that?" he asked.

"She doesn't know," Miss Nellie turned to him and put the last word in. "No one knows about heaven, Eli. That's the only good thing about dying. You get to find out what happens when you die."

THE NEXT NOVEMBER Naylor got to find out. He went out to his little house behind the kitchen and he lay down on his bed and went to sleep with all his clothes on because he was so tired he couldn't take them off. Then he didn't wake up and we don't know what happens next because no one gets to find out about dying while they are alive.

He was buried next to Margaret and her mother and all three of her mother's husbands and then a whole world was either dead or walking around heaven either thinking about things or hungry or not hungry or busy watching us to see what we are doing.